Animals at the End of the World

LATIN AMERICAN
LITERATURE IN
TRANSLATION SERIES

OTHER BOOKS IN THE SERIES

The Enlightened Army by David Toscana
Human Matter: A Fiction by Rodrigo Rey Rosa
The Last Days of El Comandante by Alberto Barrera Tyszka

Animals at the End of the World

Gloria Susana Esquivel

Translated by Robin Myers

UNIVERSITY OF TEXAS PRESS

Austin

Animales del fin del mundo copyright © 2017 by Gloria Susana Esquivel
c/o Indent Literary Agency
www.indentagency.com
Translation copyright © 2020 by Robin Myers
All rights reserved
Printed in the United States of America

Project editor: Lynne Chapman
Cover design: Isaac Tobin
Interior typesetting: Cassandra Cisneros
Typeset in Spectral
Book cover printed by Phoenix Color, interior printed by Sheridan Books

♾ The paper used in this book meets the minimum requirements of
ANSI/NISO Z39.48-1992 (R1997) (Permanence of Paper).

Library of Congress Cataloging-in-Publication Data

Names: Esquivel, Gloria Susana, author. | Myers, Robin, 1987–, translator.
Title: Animals at the end of the world / Gloria Susana Esquivel ; translated by Robin Myers.
Other titles: Animales del fin del mundo. English
Description: Austin : University of Texas Press, 2020. | Series: Latin American literature in
　　translation series
Identifiers: LCCN 2019034300
ISBN 978-1-4773-2016-7 (paperback)
ISBN 978-1-4773-2124-9 (library ebook)
ISBN 978-1-4773-2125-6 (non-library ebook)
Subjects: LCSH: Girls—Fiction. | Imagination—Fiction. | Fear—Fiction. | Colombian
　　fiction—21st century.
Classification: LCC PQ8180.415.S69 A7213 2020 | DDC 863/.7—dc23
LC record available at https://lccn.loc.gov/2019034300

doi:10.7560/320167

And one shall say unto him,
What are these wounds in thine hands?
Then he shall answer,
Those with which I was wounded in
the house of them that loved me.

ZECHARIAH 13:6

Like a small bird sealed off from daylight:
that was my childhood.

LOUISE GLÜCK

Animals at the End of the World

I

1

The year I met María, the world was predicted to end.

The news often broadcast special programs featuring numerologists and astrologists who presented their hypotheses on the exact date and time of the earth's annihilation. My dad tried to calm me down over the phone: it was only an eclipse, he'd explain, and it was only going to switch off the sky, just for a moment, just for a few seconds. Maybe we could watch it together.

Forty people killed themselves in California: they chose phenobarbital as their vehicle for evacuating the planet. A large family depleted a small German village's entire supply of canned goods in the dead of winter, forcing their neighbors to trek to the next town for provisions and prompting a few cases of hypothermia. An old Australian man sold all his property and spent six months outdoors; he slept on a mattress and ate buckets of fried chicken as he waited for an asteroid to obliterate him.

Here, though, nobody paid much attention to the apocalyptic rumors. There were other things to worry about.

At home, no one was troubled but me. I shook every time I heard the news, and I'd ask Mom, whispering, to talk with my grandparents and Julia so we'd have a contingency plan in case something went wrong. We'd build a makeshift shelter in the living room, we'd flee to the coast in the family car. But she never took me seriously. Instead of reacting to my wake-up call, she'd gently grip me by the back of the neck and start shaping my hair into new styles. I'd stand very still as my mom inserted ribbons and adjusted headbands, and, frustrated, I'd let my gaze drift far away. I couldn't believe she'd decided to ignore the possibility of us all getting crushed by a meteor.

I was six years old and I'd lost two teeth.

Whenever I tried to speak with my mother about the end of the world, she'd burst out laughing. It was one of the rare occasions when her tight, absent expression would soften and she'd seem to relax a little. She'd plant kisses all over the top of my head and then she'd get very serious and ask me to please repeat the whole anxious list to my grandparents, who were dying to hear my voice. But her cajoling was in vain. As soon as I'd learned to talk, I'd also resolved to spare myself as many conversations as possible. Back then, I remember, words felt like cold leeches wriggling around in my belly. Every time I prepared to say them out loud, I'd feel sharp cramps scaling my back. To avoid this uncomfortable sensation, I learned that I needed only my fingers to communicate. I also learned that the only important conversations were the ones I had with my mother, who was always eager to give me whatever I needed from the outside world, and the few I had with my father, when he called on the phone. Besides, I loved the silence—my own silence— that kept my eyes wide open and allowed me to register any imminent danger in my surroundings.

Silence sharpened my senses and alerted me to every sign of oncoming catastrophe. Like the possible expansion of the cosmos. Or the irrevocable aging of the stars. Or the latent threat of the sun deciding to gobble us up.

That's exactly what happened one day around seven in the morning.

Julia was singing as she carried out the arduous task of cleaning the marble floors downstairs, and my grandmother was trying to decide between three potential outfits. My grandfather was taking a shower and my mother was making breakfast.

I was asleep.

My grandfather closed his eyes as he received a final jet of cold water onto his head. Julia whistled. Mom rose from the table and took a few steps toward the fridge. My grandmother, indecisive, regarded a dark blue dress she'd carefully laid out on the bed.

The violent crash expelled me from my slumber.

Mom didn't feel the ground move, so she ruled out an earthquake. Right before her eyes, the skylights that formed the kitchen ceiling suddenly groaned and darkened with cement dust and glass powder tumbling down. The tiles parted and abandoned all horizontality; they hung down like stalactites in a cave, winged, suspended mere centimeters above her head. My grandmother's blackbirds, which had been sleeping in their cage above the table in the breakfast nook, flapped in a frenzy. They shrieked and rattled, turning the disaster scene into a cacophony of birdcalls. My grandmother ran down the stairs and the metal steps thundered under her feet, echoing the roar we'd heard. All I managed to do was get out of bed.

My grandfather emerged from the shower and appeared in the kitchen, stark naked, not noticing that the chill of the morning and the adrenaline rush had transformed his thick dark skin into a thrumming, goose-pimpled, gelatinous mass. I made my way toward the kitchen. The only noise came from the blackbirds' clattering cage, the iron bars clanging again and again.

That's the sound of the cosmos whetting its appetite. A stomach rumble foretold our death.

I took in the scene with resignation. My grandmother was crying in a corner of the room. Dumbfounded, Mom gaped up at the hole that had ruptured overhead.

My grandfather was trembling.

From where I stood, I discovered I could glimpse his testicles through a small gap between his pelvis and the towel he'd grabbed to cover himself. Fascinated, I stared at the wrinkled bulb that hung between his legs, as if I were spying on the neighbors' mysterious habits through a peephole.

I felt the urge to move closer and touch it.

The house smelled of sulfur. The air grew heavy with my grandmother's sobs, which were interrupted when my grandfather, still half-naked, plucked me up from the floor and carried me out of the house. We made our way down the spiral stairs, through halls and corridors, and reached the door in one long stride. Alarmed, he asked the neighbors and Julia, who'd been pacing uneasily along the front sidewalk for a good while, what had happened. No one seemed to understand where it had come from, this noise that had mimicked the force of a torrent breaching a dam. One of the men took out a small radio so we could listen to the news. I was the only one who seemed to grasp that a galactic typhoon was on its way. The pavement chafed my feet.

Is the sky going to fall? asked a listless voice that belonged to the only other little girl amid the group of baffled grown-up men.

No one else heard her murmur. No one else heard María. Her words were overtaken by a voice that issued weakly through the transistor static. It said something about five hundred kilos of dynamite hidden in a garbage truck.

2

I lived with my mother in my grandparents' house: a confusing Chinese box where I frittered away the infinite hours of childhood playing hide-and-seek with myself.

My grandparents had moved to the city three decades before with enough capital to expand their business. They bought the house, which at the time was an archetype of the modern architecture invading the city. They decorated it in strict accordance with the catalogues, and they never worried about whether long leather couches or faux wood finishing on every kitchen cabinet and appliance would ever be fashionable again. There they raised their six children: three boys and three girls, who constantly rebelled against the subtle stasis that their parents had imposed on them.

Nothing and no one aged in that house: not the furniture, not Julia, not my grandparents. My uncles, on the other hand, spent their childhoods and youths papering the desk in their shared bedroom with stickers from World Cup albums they patiently collected every four years, and they searched Müller's weathered face for any evidence that time had actually passed. Meanwhile, my mother and her sisters devoted themselves to collecting dozens of suitors, who would walk back and forth in front of the house, waiting for my grandfather to step out so they could sneak into that strange museum. For three decades, the children moved around like restless particles, resisting repose. They started and finished their studies, acquired and abandoned vices, formed and splintered families, made all the wise and ill-fated decisions it was possible to make inside the house. Then they left and never came back.

Except for Mom. She did come back. After her marriage ended and she lost her job as a flight attendant, she reappeared on the doorstep of her childhood home, baby in tow, and asked my grandmother for help in raising me. And so I started growing up inside this strange, infinite labyrinth, observing my mother's long siestas under the silence and heavy surveillance of my grandparents and Julia.

On the second floor were the three bedrooms that my aunts and uncles once shared, gradually left vacant as each one made his or her escape. I reconquered these territories. Rarely visited by my grandparents, this part of the house was more like a cemetery for incomplete furniture. It was there that I learned to play alone, accompanied by nothing but a bed base with no mattress that no one had ever reclaimed, collecting the bits of fluff that accumulated on the empty, sloping shelves of an unstable library.

My grandfather's studio, the kitchen, and my grandmother's deck were also located on this floor. Their ceilings were all glass, which meant that you could always see the color of the sky. The bedroom I shared with my mother was right next to the kitchen, and we were wakened every morning by Grandma's blackbirds. You could only reach the deck by cutting across the kitchen, and you could only go up to my grandparents' bedroom, on the third floor, by cutting across the deck. In this way, our room, the blackbirds' room, and my grandparents' room were connected like a set of residential train cars that sequestered us from the vastness of the house.

Downstairs was another world and never a wholly familiar one. Every corner of the first floor contained a secret, a nook, a cupboard, a hallway, or a staircase that didn't seem to lead anywhere at all. The front door opened onto a bone-white hall where my grandparents hosted their parties. A chandelier, hung with hundreds of tear-shaped crystals that swayed menacingly overhead, gleamed onto a mottled stone floor. The walls were draped with enormous tapestries depicting romantic Indian scenes: abducted princesses, shirtless musicians strumming their lyres, prancing dancers, all lit by the white light winking out from the glass tears overhead. A record player occupied one corner of the hall; atop it was the horrible collection of porcelain clowns that my grandmother sometimes offered me as extras in the games starring my dolls. Behind this space was a series of corridors, vectors that connected the first-floor rooms. And all of those rooms were faded copies of the vast white entrance hall: the only difference was the size of the tapestries, the lamp, and the clowns, which were randomly smaller or larger in each of the subsequent rooms. But their arrangement was always designed as a macabre mirror of the first.

No matter how many times I wandered the hallways, something kept me from remembering which corridor led to which corner, which cranny, which room. Whenever I turned a doorknob, I felt the surging anxiety of an unpleasant surprise. Searching for the guest room, for example, I'd find myself in the middle of my grandmother's sewing room. My greatest fear was the thought that, just as each room was a tattered copy of the main hall, the house might also contain different copies of me.

I imagined stumbling across another fragile little

blonde girl behind one of those doors. Her skin was gray and dry. Her pupils were albino-blank. She lived in one of the first-floor rooms. She was one of my doubles and I was terrified that I might encounter her someday. But despite my fear, I played at trying to find her. I suspected that this particular nightmare encoded one of the house's greatest secrets, and I knew I'd have to be brave and look the other girl in the eyes, which were also my eyes. I tiptoed down the hall, not making a sound, so she wouldn't sense me creeping up on her. Maybe she was in the guests' living room or hidden deep inside my grandparents' liquor cabinet. I approached with the silence of a huntress patiently studying her prey, and I slipped around the corners where I suspected she might be lurking. Sometimes my grandmother caught me in this game of single-player hide-and-seek, and she shouted at me to break the trance: Inés! Stop crawling around on the floor. You're wrinkling your dress. *Those aren't games for a little girl.* And I fled to the second floor, relieved, abandoning any chance of encountering my gloomy reflection, at least for that day.

Julia's bedroom was also located in one of those confusing parts of the house. It was a large space completely crammed with furniture, and it had a bathroom and one of the few windows that looked onto the outside world. The two beds, bedside tables, dresser, and desk that occupied the room, all jigsaw-puzzled around each other, were transformed during the day as she went about her household tasks. They became mountainous paths or colossal boulders I scaled to seek refuge from a floor that I imagined as covered in lava, or boogers, and which I forbade myself from touching with my feet. On her windowsill were various flowerpots filled with Peruvian lilies and petunias that shone in the midday light as it spread across the yellow walls—the only glimpse of color I remember on the first floor of the house. This made her bedroom one of my favorite places, especially when it stopped raining. I'd sprawl out in the sun, imagining that my body was covered with little purple membranes, and I'd follow the current of my dream in hopes that I'd wake metamorphosed into a lily, and then I'd practice meticulously moving my fingers, which were now leaves and petals, like a set of pincers to entrap flies, dust, and any other object that dared drift close to me.

I was Inés, decorative plant. Inés, house pet. Inés, porcelain animal, lost in the infinite recesses of the house and its silence.

The house was also inhabited by the beast, which always woke when I wasn't paying attention. Sometimes, when I was hiding from my double, I'd get disoriented in the corridor that led to one of the sewing rooms, open the wrong door, and find myself face to face with it. Furious. Panting. Demanding silence and cursing the fact that it couldn't find peace in its own house. I'd close the door very carefully and carry on with my games, leaving the beast to its rage, knowing it was best to leave it alone. After all, since I didn't speak beast, any word or gesture of mine could be misinterpreted and unleash roars and thumps that would leave my knees trembling.

No matter how hard I tried to study its behavior or anticipate its attacks, it remained utterly unpredictable to me. Julia saw its wrath as a runaway horse galloping furiously over the hills, never gauging the speed and strength of its hoofs, stopping only when it found a place to rest. She shrewdly counseled me to get out of its way whenever I heard it snort and shout about important papers, my messy room, or how ridiculous it was that a girl my age didn't talk. Unintelligible reproofs. Muffled bellows in what sounded to me like a foreign language.

If I was unlucky enough to cross its path, it would bare its teeth and unhinge its jaw. It would bring its canines very close to my face and threaten to swallow me up. I could sense its insatiable hunger for my flesh.

It salivated.

It was enormous.

Rabid.

Poised to attack.

Strong enough to snatch me into the air with a single swipe and rattle my bones.

It seemed incensed by my very presence. It howled and flashed its terrible teeth, ready to snap at my fingers, and I quickly dropped my gaze, terrified that it would trap me in its jaws.

When we gathered at the table, the beast bristled at how slowly I ate and sat close beside me, teeming with impatience. It gripped spoonfuls of rice or soup in its beast-hands and fed me violently. The metal struck and scraped the roof of my mouth, and I gagged against the mass of food. I hurried to swallow my disgust, awaiting the next swiftly approaching spoonful. If I froze or threw up a little, the beast would grunt with exasperation and stalk off: I was a lost cause, it would shout. Or it would seize the plate and toss it over my head, engulfing me in pasta sauce or oatmeal, and sit there staring at me. Maybe it expected me to talk back, to yell, to reach out and give it a thwack. But I felt paralyzed by its rage, and

I'd just fix my gaze on something in the kitchen, my belly cold and quivering.

I collected my fear in my mouth, along the edge of my loosest teeth, and I stifled my screams. I accepted its smacks and clouts. Some on the head. Others on my body. And I imagined myself completely sheathed in firm, hard-wearing, copper-plated armor, a full-body shield that could cushion any blow. The metal plates resounded with every muted shout. They transformed the blows into a conspiratorial echo that rumbled through the house like thunder.

But there were other times when the beast and I kept each other company in silence. It stroked my head with clumsy hands as it drank long swigs of whiskey, holding them in its mouth, as in the crop of a giant bird, before releasing the drink to warm its throat. And then it swallowed with a great popping sound and a rush of bitter wood-breath, a sharp smell that mingled with the scent of its aftershave. When it was feeling generous or cheerful, it would offer me a sip, too, insisting that it would soothe the ache in my baby teeth. I'd timidly accept. The alcohol roiled my stomach and made me feel sick. The beast patted me on the back, praising my courage, and took my face into its gargantuan paws to shake it like a snow globe. Laughing, it told me that it had a piece of string in its pocket and it was going to tie one end around the doorknob and the other around my teeth so that they'd all jump out at once and I'd finally be able to show off a new smile. Then it gave me a kiss that coated my cheeks with its sour spittle and walked away, slowly, whistling, paws clasped behind its back.

No matter what sort of state he was in, these moments with my grandfather always left me flooded with a feeling of uncertainty that became a tepid stream of pee I'd allow to escape over my shoes and relieve my fear.

The warm drops would soak through my underpants before they fled and trickled down my legs. It was a yellow pain. Exquisite.

Deep.

3

We weren't outside for long after the explosion. Prisoners to a rash and curious spirit, we returned to the house and peered into the kitchen to assess the disaster. That's where Mom was, hyperactive, frenzied, shaking her head as if she were finally waking up from a long hypnosis. She inspected me carefully to make sure I was intact; my father had called to check up on me and she wanted to confirm that everything was in order.

My grandmother felt her blood pressure dropping and sat down on a dining room chair that was lightly coated with debris-dust. Since Mom was in the kitchen when the explosion hit, she was the only one who'd been injured. She had shallow cuts on her cheeks and a deeper gash across her right eyebrow. A thick line of blood trickled all the way down her feline cheekbone and weak chin. With the diligence she'd learned in her emergency training class, she opened the first-aid kit and washed herself, sewed herself up, and calmed herself down. As if the face looking back at her from the mirror were the face of a passenger who was terrified of heights and had to be distracted in a moment of powerful turbulence.

Shyly, Julia also entered the kitchen and Mom pounced on her, checking her pupils and reflexes. Julia laughed at every instruction. She told Mom she was just fine; she'd only heard a loud bang on the first floor, not unlike the dull thud emitted by the clogged exhaust pipe of a city bus. The blackbirds had stopped flapping. They screeched with their heads tucked into their wings, bodies transformed into feathered hearts, palpitating uneasily. I watched the birds from the doorway, unaware that I'd shrunk with terror, too. Frozen on the threshold, I feared that the world would threaten to end again if I moved. And as I stood there, distracted by my own terror, someone patted me on the back, a touch I can still feel like the electric charge of a thousand eels.

Startled, I turned around and saw María.

Julia, pressed for an explanation, hurried to tell my grandmother why this other girl had come inside, but the old woman narrowed her cold, impatient eyes at me.

Ignoring the chill that her presence had provoked, María took my hand and asked me to show her all my *rich-kid toys*. I was flummoxed: she was the first child I'd seen in a long time and I wasn't sure how to act. Inés, fawn, would sniff her ears and knuckles and break the ice. But before my double could give herself over to instinct, María was pulling me toward my bedroom to play hair salon with my dolls.

As if possessed by a woman in heels, María began to imitate a solicitous voice, welcoming clients to the beauty salon. With her right hand clutching mine and her left gripping Natalia Josefa's blonde head, we darted into the bathroom, where we unabashedly turned on the faucets of the sink that now served as our hair-washing station.

"But heavens, ma'am, how could you possibly let this little girl's hair get so dirty! My goodness. My stars. What she has is lice, you see? We'll need to apply a special product," she said, as she selected some of the miniature heart-shaped, fruity-smelling soaps my grandmother used to decorate the bathroom and scanned the sink for any other scented things. She began to scrub the doll's head vigorously. Its eyelids opened and shut with every energetic movement. I could hear my grandmother in the kitchen, reprimanding Julia for her indiscretion, interrupting herself to shout that we shouldn't be playing with water. But it was as if María couldn't hear the reproaches at all. She seized a handful of Kleenex and crushed them onto Natalia Josefa's head. The stoic doll tolerated this brusque treatment.

With María's arrival, my house would never be mute again.

We started to draw. I drew a big, dark sun, using all the colors I had, just as I imagined the eclipse that my father always talked about. María scolded me because my drawings were careless and looked nothing like hers, which were composed with soft crayon-strokes and colors that bore more resemblance to reality. I drew crooked houses inhabited by green-skinned men with bears for pets, and she conjured landscapes with flowering mountainsides, rivers full of brilliant fish, birds cutting across the sky. With the radio in the background, we listened to songs about a man begging someone to *wake me up before you go-go* and Jolene, who was going to steal some other woman's man.

María had brought a small red Ninja Turtles backpack that contained her most valuable possessions: two jars of plastic stick-on jewels she liked affixing to her belly with Vaseline and which made her feel like one of the presenters of the Saturday morning kids' competition show on Peruvian TV; a too-small plastic pearl necklace; a box of bright watercolors she used to paint her face; a little tulle bag full of rocks and uncooked rice, which was helpful to us when we pretended to make dinner; and a mirror with a drawing of the main character of a French animated doll show on the back.

That afternoon, we also played with Laura Carolina, my favorite doll, and Angélica Susana, her favorite. We imagined they lived in a house without any boyfriends or husbands, just lots of clothes to iron. At a certain point in the game, a catastrophe was unleashed and the house burned down, or a car bomb exploded, as it had that very morning. We had to flee with our daughters, first toward the pool and then toward the snow. When we finally managed to settle elsewhere, far from the threats we'd escaped, we started working at a restaurant or a travel agency, where we scribbled checks and traded collectible cards that served as ultra-valuable million-peso bills.

Sometimes the beast, furious, interrupted our games and demanded that we make less noise. Sometimes my grandmother was the one who called me over to talk with her and told me crisply that she didn't think it was appropriate for me to lend María my dolls, that I should make sure nothing was missing once she'd gone home. I didn't pay her much attention. I returned to my room, ready to answer the question that would become María's perennial greeting—what are we going to do now?—as if I alone were responsible for the wild, delirious oscillation of that afternoon with her.

As I played with María, I saw the silhouettes of several men who'd come to fix the roof. They removed the tiles and laid thick tarps over the hole in the kitchen as a temporary solution. I remember my grandmother surrounded by friends who'd come to play cards, and my grandfather howling orders, stalking in and out of his study all afternoon. I also remember this as the day when, for the first time in years, Mom went out and came back, astonished by everything she'd seen outside. She was so amazed that she smiled, sang, and sniffed at locks of her own hair, going on about how much she liked the smell of dry gasoline that had suffused the whole city—and her.

In the evening, after María had left, my bedsheets felt as heavy as wooden boards. I wriggled around, trying to shake off their suffocating weight. Mom wanted to sleep in my bed and sing *boleros* to calm me down. I burrowed my nose into her neck and took a thick length of her ponytail into my mouth. I let her melancholy song lull me into drowsiness as I felt her hair between my lips and tried to figure out what the city tasted like.

I didn't understand what had happened that day: the explosion, María, her games . . . it all unsettled me. Half asleep, I was flooded with questions about whether the sky was going to crash down onto us at last. Because now, for the first time, I had a friend. Together, I was sure we'd be able to defend ourselves from the hungry cosmos, from the blows of the beast, from my double life, from my grandparents' cavernous house. I turned these ideas around in my head again and again. Just before I fell asleep, I was struck by a thunderous intuition. Maybe it was time to make a new home. María, my father, my mother, and me: we'd all be there. We wouldn't need my grandparents anymore. The blackbirds would no longer hysterically trumpet the end of the world.

I wouldn't be afraid of anything.

4

My father's face was different every time he came to see me. Sometimes he had a dark mustache that made him look like a ridiculous movie star. Or sometimes his hair had grown and a few gray strands peeked out shyly from his dark black mane. Or he'd suddenly decided to wear aviator sunglasses that made him look very dashing, or he'd grown out his beard and ended up looking like a crooner from another era. I didn't always recognize him. To make sure I did, my strategy was to focus on his hands, which were the only things that didn't change. Large and rough, the backs covered in sunspots, they looked like the large, mottled shells of the tortoises we saw in a pet store one day when he took me downtown for a doctor's appointment. On the rare occasions when I saw him, I always fantasized that this time we'd finally run off and be together forever. Before leaving the house, I'd go to my bedroom and say a silent goodbye to each and every one of my toys, promising I'd come back for them soon. I'd rush down the stairs, hoping to find the other Inés who lived on the ground floor and tell her I was leaving for good; as a peace offering, I wanted to propose that she could go live on the first floor, so my mom and grandparents wouldn't miss me too much. I'd leave the house, beaming, and get into his car, and I'd rest my head in his lap and doze as he deftly shifted his feet on the pedals.

We always spent the whole afternoon outside the city, because Dad liked taking me places where I could be around animals. When we were together, my father would stretch out facedown in the grass and ask me to walk on his back. With steady tightrope-walker feet, I'd knead his buttocks with my feet and step along his spine, all the way up to his shoulder blades and back again. My father's body was a path—sometimes firm, sometimes soft—that I had to tread with care. When he wanted the massage to stop, he'd wriggle around and try to shake me off. And when I fell, he'd gather me up in his arms, fuss over me with brusque tenderness, set me down on my back, and tickle me from my belly to my neck. He'd take his time ascending my body with his fingers, as if he enjoyed prolonging my agony. I'd be transformed into a single happy spasm, thrashing against his touch. Laughing helplessly, I'd try to grab his fingers and hold them under my chin to stop the onslaught. And then he'd manage to wrest his hands away and continue, unleashing a powerful cackle from my insides that clung to the walls of my belly and threatened to choke the air out of me altogether. When I found myself on the verge of suffocation, he'd lean down and plant kisses all over me. Gentle ones on my forehead that turned into quick, insistent pecks on my skull. He'd take me by the neck, bring his cheeks close to mine, and start to brush my skin with his beard-bristles. Sometimes he'd grab my neck much harder, and in the thrill of the game he wouldn't realize that he was hurting me. I'd fix my lips to his neck and slobber all over him. When I couldn't take it anymore, I'd sink my teeth into his flesh.

Then Dad would stop and we'd both collapse with laughter.

I was his and his alone.

My father's skin tasted like salt.

Later, around nightfall, we'd return to my grandparents' house. Half asleep, half awake, I'd follow planes flashing across the sky until they disappeared from view. Back at the front gate, I'd cling to him like a tick and hope he'd tell me not to ever let him go, that we'd sleep in the same bed tonight, that his body would become my new home. He'd ring the bell and wait for Julia to untangle the skein of keys that opened every lock of every gate protecting the maternal fortress, and he'd deliver me, flailing, raging, wild, into her arms. He'd turn and walk away, get into his car, and switch on the headlights, and I'd watch the night swallow him up as he was lost to me.

5

After the explosion, Mom seemed electrified by a new energy. She darted around the house, left, came back, and went out again, frenetic and restless and loud as a hornet. During one of those enthusiastic to-and-fros, she persuaded my grandparents to let Julia bring María to play with me at least once a week.

Now I understand that what I felt was anxiety. As I awaited the next time I'd see my new friend, my chest would fill with burbles I could only expel with a giggle attack. All I could think of was María and her games. Of how she'd lined up all my stuffed animals in fours to play bus, and how she'd then rearranged them in a circle to pretend she was the owner of a café and had to wait on them meticulously. I also laughed every time I remembered the jokes and riddles she'd told me that first day, and how before I could even repeat them to my grandmother I'd felt the crush of laughter amassing in my throat, a ruthless river that would drag me along with its gleeful current and make me ask Julia about her granddaughter. Julia was so excited to hear me talking, finally, that she'd said nothing about María. Instead, she'd pronounced random phrases very slowly and asked me to repeat them, scripted and deliberate as a language-learning tape.

Mom could tell that María was good for me. She was amazed by my laughter, by my attempts at conversation with Julia, and by my brand-new courage—acquired in a matter of days—that coaxed me out of the house to run errands with my grandmother, unimpeded by my own terror at the ferocious creatures parading along the sidewalk. I had even stopped wetting the bed.

The explosion had changed her, too. She looked much more awake, now that she was leaving the house, her face newly bright and glowing.

For the past couple of years, my mother's routine had consisted entirely of naps and long baths behind closed doors. My grandmother asked me to go in every hour and a half to check how much longer she would be. What I found on the other side of the door was a fragile body made of pins and cardboard—or at least that's what she looked like—that shivered in the tub. I looked at her silently and sat down beside her until she got up and walked from the bathroom to our bedroom, wrapped in a towel, leaving faint watery footprints on the floor tiles.

Mom would spend the rest of the day braiding my hair and watching soap operas, or telling me stories I received with rapt attention. I imagined the day we'd go live with my father. From that day forward, he'd be the one stretched out beside us, listening to these fantastical stories. We lay down and looked at each other, my mother and I, and the bed became a warm place that sheltered me from fear. My mom told me about a girl whose name was also Inés, but she was a princess in a faraway country. She never cried, which was how she'd managed to become the fairest and most beautiful in all the land. She also told me about the princes who dueled for her love, and how the princess was a big girl because she always ate everything on the plate in front of her. Sometimes she ran out of Inés stories and so she told me about her own childhood instead: the rough games she played with her brothers, her sisters' teenage secrets, the missions she had to fulfill at work, the times she'd nearly died.

Perhaps as a warning, she kept telling me different versions of her first brush with death, in case I ever neglected to look both ways before crossing the narrow avenues that flanked the house. When she was seven years old, a truck had snatched her away from her mother as they walked along an uncrowded street in a warm city where they used to go on vacation. It seems that my grandmother had been momentarily distracted by a brawl across the street and rushed toward the ruckus at the wrong time. Mom felt nothing. She woke in a hospital where the nurses spoiled her and plied her with Jell-O; she spent three months there, watching black-and-white variety shows in bed. That first near-miss left her with a fondness for the smell of plaster and an enormous scar on her right side that I liked to touch when she was in the bath. It was stiff and rough. I believed for a long time that the snakes invading Inés's kingdom when she was bad were just like my mother's scar: knots of dry flesh that slithered along under the princess's bed and threatened to gnaw at her heels.

Mom had another long scar on her pubic bone that she never let me touch. Many years later, I'd learn that she had an emergency operation at sixteen because she tried to abort a pregnancy by drinking a thick, corrosive liquid—made of weeds, burnt hair, and ethyl alcohol—that a witch doctor had prescribed her. It worked, insofar as it did away with the cells that would have otherwise become a fetus, but it also perforated her intestine. My mother mistook the fever and cramps for side effects of the concoction. One of her sisters found her in the bathroom, passed out from the pain, and ran to find their parents. At the clinic, the doctors learned that her intestine was about to burst and release a fatal torrent of pus and infected matter into her bloodstream. As a consequence of her second near-death experience, she lost part of her digestive tract and gained an intense phobia of vomiting.

Her third run-in with mortality was just after her twenty-eighth birthday, when she made a last-minute decision to switch shifts with one of her coworkers so she could skip the morning flight. She'd been working as a flight attendant for four years and she was tired. She'd never allowed herself a single license, liberty, or concession. Any action that could possibly suggest a weakness of character, she believed, would result in the loss of her job, her life, and her independence. She told my father all of this over the phone, and he listened unenthused. They'd been dating for a few months and this was the first time she'd ever made herself even remotely vulnerable. Mom thought he was being indifferent. Dad heard her words as heavy, amorphous, slow-moving sounds that seeped into his hangover after a long night out. Mom erupted with rage and decided she didn't want to be with him anymore. They were done. They weren't going to hole up that weekend in a motel in the north of the city, as they had planned. They weren't going to share endless hours of junk food and porn. But she wasn't going to tell him she'd decided to stand him up—she wanted him to find out the hard way.

Her scheduled flight exploded at thirteen thousand feet. So did my father's heart when he heard the news. Two days passed before he gathered up the nerve to call my grandparents' house. He learned that she was safe and sound. He also learned that she'd left the city and was staying at a hotel, finally using the vacation days she'd so longed for. She'd barely dodged death—again—and felt that she had to go somewhere far away. She didn't say a word for three weeks. And she didn't want to give him any evidence of her survival. She thought about the agony he must feel, not knowing where she was, and she relished it. He was the one who'd have to look for her. And as soon as he found her, he proposed. He wanted to protect her, to barricade them against accidents. Imprisoned by euphoria, she said yes. I am the product of her third near-death experience. I wreathed my mother's belly and thighs with stretch marks, scraped the walls of her vagina and perineum, and brought her the perpetual anguish of never knowing what to do with a little girl who depended on her, and on her alone, to survive.

6

Those were also the days when Mom stopped sleeping at home.

When she was gone, I was the queen of her kingdom.

Sometimes I stole her makeup and María and I applied it to the faces of my dolls, trying to imitate Mom's daintiness in adorning her own. We plastered them with blush, lipstick, and eye shadow, and then we lined them up like a legion of spectators who'd come to watch us dance. Other times we plunged into her closet and tried on dresses and sweaters that still smelled like her. María and I put on her shoes and walked all around the house, dragging what we thought was adulthood in our wake. Our goal was to make ourselves irresistible, like the women in the evening soaps. That's why we had to walk in a straight line, skirting the geometric patterns of the kitchen tiles.

Whenever Julia saw us playing, she scolded María and threatened to never bring her back to my house again if she kept grabbing the boss's things without permission. I laughed at María when she scowled, elongating my neck and straightening my shoulders, proud of how I looked in my mother's clothes. I didn't think Julia was being serious, because once she was finished berating María she asked if I was hungry and brought me a snack to eat at the side table, setting down a plate of French fries, peanuts, fruit, and chocolates in front of me. She took a package of cookies out of her purse and held it out to her granddaughter. I left my snack half-eaten and didn't share with my friend.

María's favorite singer was Juan Luis Guerra. She wanted us to listen to his tape all the time, and we ended up learning all the songs on the A side and some on the B side, too. It was music for kissing, or at least that's what she said. We shut ourselves in my bedroom and sprawled out on a makeshift bed of sheets we arranged on the floor as we listened to the rain falling onto the hills. Each of us hugged a teddy bear close to our bodies and stared steadily into its eyes, like we were in love. We wanted to re-create the scenes in soap operas when the stars clung to each other and kissed furiously. When those scenes came on TV, I was overwhelmed by an urge to sit on the edge of the bed, plant my hands close to my hips, cross my legs hard, and rock back and forth until a pleasant sensation pulled me toward sleep. Clutching my teddy bear, I felt the same warm flutter curling up from my lower back. María brought a hand to her mouth and started to lick it, her tongue like a deft little salmon flapping against the current.

She closed her eyes and her feet swayed to the beat of the downpour.

Our toes touched under the sheets. I stared at the thin sky-blue cotton undershirt that framed her shoulders, and I envied her underpants, which were printed with the days of the week.

I licked her armpits. They smelled like talcum powder.

She rolled onto me and we became a tangle of legs, arms, and drowning tongues. We were Siamese twins, linked at the head, and with each brusque movement, each attempt to unravel ourselves, I felt a sharp yank that rattled my teeth.

The spasms were a quiet throb.

Placid.

Red . . .

Thrilling.

A suffocation pulsing near the thighs.

María and I found some masks that someone had forgotten in one of the house's countless drawers. Hers was
white velvet and it had a pointy snout, a pair of tiny cat-
ears, and two holes for eyes that intensified her deep, wild
gaze. Mine was metallic and covered with gray feathers
and had a very long beak. On the upper part, it had two
huge polystyrene balls covered in yellow sequins, creating the illusion that my eyes had been swallowed up by
a pair of radiant bird-orbs. When we put on the masks,
we were transformed. María, girl-panther, would pounce
on me and try to trap me in her claws. Her attacks were
fierce; she hit me hard. She was aggressive and ruthless
and therefore exceptionally good at this game. She always
took advantage of me. But I became light and graceful as
a girl-crow. I watched her severely, gauging her movements. Whenever the panther lunged at me, I unhesi-
tatingly bit, poked, and pecked at her arms, scratching
her skin and leaving it imprinted with my teeth. Then I
flapped my wings and vanished into the house's cavernous nooks and crannies.

I felt powerful beside her, flying around the ground
floor.

I wasn't afraid of the house anymore.

I'd lost my third tooth.

Still in disguise, we decided to sketch a map of the house.
Like military strategists, we came up with a methodical
plan to conquer and occupy various territories I would

have never dared to enter without my friend. Key targets included the laundry room, the second-floor bathroom cabinets, and my grandfather's study. This last place was one of my favorites. I loved to lie down under his hulking oak desk and transform the space into the perfect office, a refuge where I could draw and listen to music without anyone bothering me. I had to do this very carefully, since one of the things the beast hated most was finding hints of me among his possessions. And even though Mom had asked me a million times to not go in there, sometimes she spent the afternoon in the tub and left me alone with Julia, and so I'd sneak off with a kids' encyclopedia from some forgotten library and spend hours sitting under that desk, looking at drawings of ballet moves and Christmas traditions all over the globe.

I knew almost all the secrets of the office: where the little blue bars of mounting putty were (I liked to pinch the corners and shape them into tiny balls and chew on them), how the papers were organized, the different kinds of pencils my grandfather used to mark up the accounting documents for his company. I'd memorized all the corners of the drawers and learned how to nose around the mountains of stationary supplies without leaving a trace. But what I found most unnerving about that mysterious lair was a closet that was always locked with a key I'd never found. It seemed that no one had ever opened that door, so jealously guarded by its invisible key. Not even Mom. Julia didn't know what my grandfather kept in there either, because he'd never told her how to clean and organize its contents.

Now, years later, I find myself remembering the afternoons I spent rummaging around in there, peering into every crack, trying to guess which key would open the enigmatic door. I'd get so engrossed in the search that I sometimes forgot to cover my tracks. Maybe my double lived inside that closet, or maybe it was where a family secret was buried. Maybe it contained an object that would prove the house wasn't my house at all; maybe some fluke had kept me from living the life I was meant to live. Then the beast would roar into the study and unleash his force on me. To prevent further trouble, my grandmother had decided to keep the room itself under lock and key. Armed with my mask and accompanied by María, though, I felt that nothing could keep me from recovering this forbidden territory. I needed to find the truth I'd been denied, the truth awaiting me behind the closet door.

I was Inés, secret bird. Inés, strategist. Inés, invincible crow's beak, who would tear down the forbidden door with the help of her friend, the mighty panther.

Poised at the end of the corridor, María and I geared up and hurtled down the hall, trying to gain enough speed to collide with the wooden door and destroy it with our bodies. Me first, then her. We alternated our crashes like waves breaking onto the shore, only to return again with greater force. Our arms didn't hurt, and every rebound between the door and the ground sent us into shrieks of laughter. The game continued until Julia appeared, shouting and threatening María with a broom, begging her granddaughter to behave for the sake of her job.

Then we sat down at the table and took an inventory of the bruises we'd collected on our arms, organizing them from largest to smallest. We could never agree on whether the winner was María, whose thick, dark skin camouflaged the bruises, or me, whose purpled arms looked like the mottled back of a deer.

Despite all our efforts, we never managed to open the door to my grandfather's study by flinging our bodies against it.

7

I have a photo of María and me on a swing. My body looks awkwardly arranged, wobbly, as if I were leaning against a soapy surface, and I'm making a strange face at the camera. My legs are spread. I'm not sitting like my grandmother taught me to; I'm not sitting like a lady. A long dress engulfs me from waist to ankles and a pair of cherry-red shoes hang inches from the floor, creating the illusion that I'm extraordinarily small. María firmly grips the chains of the swing. Her curls are unkempt: the only thing holding them back is a tiny yellow buckle offering heroic resistance to the entropy of her hair. She's wearing a pink sweatshirt stamped with the face of a famous Brazilian singer who used to host a children's TV show. Her spine is perfectly straight. Her dark face, broad back, and long limbs appear in stark contrast to my freckled, violet-stippled skin, my frail vertebrae. We look like a foreign-language textbook trying to explain what opposites are.

The photo is from the day my dad took us to the circus. He wanted us to see animals up close and got tickets for a show. On the way, he talked incessantly about all the big cats that would parade obediently before us. My father, wide-eyed as a child, regaled us with accounts of acrobats performing wild feats on impossible geometric structures. María and I listened, rapt, and when I saw how her face shone brighter every time my father started another story, I felt hundreds of ticks crawling up and down my throat. My jealousy was quickly drowned by a

surge of enthusiasm as I imagined the three of us trans-
forming the circus into a new house where we'd all be
curious children.

We reached the tent, which had a rickety platform
strewn with hay and several rows of plastic chairs and
beer crates that served as seats around the stage. We'd
arrived in time for the main attraction. The star was a
man who had devoted the last twelve years of his life to
taking care of and training Shir Khan, the company's old-
est Bengal tiger, and he informed us that he would use a
range of nonverbal commands to show us the majesty
and intelligence of this great beast.

Dad insisted we sit in the front row. The scent of dry
animal fur mingled with sweet gusts of caramel popcorn.
The warm trail of fragrance weakened and thrilled me.

Deftly, the tiger sprang onto a step, following his
trainer's commands. The man was dressed for a safari.
He boasted about his ability to communicate more
profoundly with animals than with humans. He spoke
their language; they were all wild animals together. He
placed his hand in the tiger's field of vision. The tiger
swiped a listless paw. It seemed like they were greeting
each other. He extended his other hand and received the
same response. Faster now, he switched his hands back
and forth. Shir Khan was a great boxing champion, he
laughed. The animal's reaction was brusque, energetic.
He seemed annoyed. He wasn't in the mood to put on a
show. The audience laughed, enraptured, clapping with
the hunger of spectators at a Roman circus. I couldn't
take my eyes off the warm feline body that thrummed in
all three dimensions before me.

It was hot, furred flesh, formidable matter.

The man dropped his hands and the tiger dropped

its tail. Then the man extended his arms and the tiger did the same. *Just like kung fu, just like kung fu! Watch him fight!* And there were shrieks and guffaws from the crowd as the speakers in the cage blared the first beats of a lively *vallenato* melody. The animal's blank gaze never wavered. His flanks sketched hypnotic patterns in the air: black and white lines across a yellow perimeter that seemed to contain a secret message just for me. I felt summoned to enter the cage, approach the tiger, take his harsh fangs into my hands, tempt his claws, climb onto his back, stretch out my body onto his. Make a new home in his two hundred kilos of muscle and brawn.

He growled. And swiped harder. Shir Khan seized his trainer by the neck and shook the man between his jaws. Dad flung an arm across my body, as if he wanted to be a barrier between the beast and my eyes. I didn't want to see anything. My hands were slick with sweat, my legs reduced to worms. I started to wail, my voice rising out of me like a river's eager torrent, willing to sink and sweep away anything that crossed its path. My eyes found María as I screamed. She was watching everything intently. Some people were evacuating the tent, others shouting for a doctor, and still others thronging in front of us, trying to rush onstage and come to the trainer's rescue. Shadows darted forth from the depths of the tent and amassed at the entrance. My cries grew louder and louder, melting into the tiger's roar, intensifying a thunder that sounded like a storm or the frenzied buzz of an angry beehive. Sometimes other shrieks competed with mine, and I tried to scream louder, like a drowning person thrashing to the surface for a gasp of air—until my weeping became a sound like María's laughter at the stories my father told us.

María, ferocious, stared at the tiger.

Amid the chaos, she never took her eyes from him.

She roared.

She looked him in the eye, and the tiger obeyed: he released his prey.

8

I gave it a lot of thought, and I concluded that the only possible explanation for the tiger's obedience to María was that she must be an animal, too. A strange kind of girl-cat who knew the secret language of felines and could communicate with them through barely perceptible gestures.

The signs were clear. Her hair was much thicker and glossier than mine, and in certain sudden rushes of light, it looked more like an animal's brown pelt than the weak tangles growing out of my scalp. A thin, dark fuzz shadowed the skin behind her ears and neck, only visible when I drew my nose close to her face in a clumsy attempt to sniff her breath for hints of cat food. Besides, my grandmother's blackbirds fluttered with panic every time she came into the kitchen. She was toothier than I was, and her teeth were sharp, and she savagely clenched my arms and hands in her strong jaws whenever she bit me.

One morning, as we played at running all over the garage without stepping on the lines that divided the tiles, I was stunned by her agility, by how seldom she had to catch her breath. My voice was very serious when I levied the charges against her. *I know you're a cat, María. Stop lying to me.*

Naturally, María mocked my words and my canary-hair. I ignored her and continued my exposition: some nights, I explained, my mom watched a TV show about a man who turned into a falcon and a bear. María turned my evidence into an invitation to play, growling impatiently.

Frustrated, I refused. I needed to understand why she ran as fast as she ran, why she never got tired during our games, why she always looked so strong. My questions made her laugh. Playing at my grandparents' house was nothing compared to the entire afternoons she spent playing soccer with her friends. Sometimes she took a bike that had once belonged to various uncles, cousins, and neighbors and rode it as far as her legs would take her. She pedaled up and down the steep hills behind her house and thought about me. She also confessed that she'd asked Julia if I could go visit her at home someday, and her grandmother had responded with an emphatic no.

I struggled to imagine the scenes María recounted to me. My grandparents never let me out alone and no one had bothered to teach me how to ride a bike. Besides, I thought everything beyond the confines of my house was dangerous; I was terrified by the very thought of the outside world. I feared the street, and it had never crossed my mind that you might play there.

My grandparents' neighborhood was full of enormous houses that had been made into restaurants, doctors' offices, and political headquarters. You very rarely glimpsed a child amid the horde of office workers and old people making their way down its streets. The closest thing to a park was a few blocks away, but it was bordered by two busy avenues, and whenever I passed it—the few times I went with Julia to the market—my knees turned to Jell-O as the pavement shuddered under the public buses that were quintuple my size. They were massive tin monsters that could squash me at any moment, tumbling my insides across the asphalt like an unlucky pigeon.

As if this weren't bad enough, a wolf lived on the

sidewalk across the street. Its feet bled. It walked with a sack slung over its shoulder and it slept on flattened cardboard boxes under the windowsill of a stationary store on the other side of the road. Its eyes were deep and gray, the color of the sky after a downpour. Whenever my grandmother and I ran into it on a walk, she'd quicken her step, clutching her purse. I hung on to her instinctively, biting my lips and lowering my eyes, overcome with fear that it would snatch both my grandmother's purse and me in a single paw-stroke.

Everything that happened outside my house made me very nervous. With every noise that surged in through the windows—a dog's bark, the hoarse roar of an engine—my bones tightened to steel and my skeleton turned into a heavy set of armor, oppressing my chest with a weight as overwhelming as when the beast lunged at me and tried to break my neck.

Once, months before, the scream of a dozen sirens broke the hush that always subsumed the house at night. The flashing lights of ambulances and police cars seeped in through the blinds, and everyone ran downstairs to see what was happening. Anxious bystanders had begun to gather around a building, the campaign headquarters of a presidential candidate. Peering out the window, I watched them pace to the beat of the wailing alarms and horns. My grandmother turned on the sound system in the main living room and tuned in to the radio. Breaking news. Gunfire. It was the third presidential candidate to suffer an assassination attempt in under six months. The voice on the radio sounded distressed and repeatedly cracked. No one knew how serious the injuries were. Everyone in my house blurted erratic speculations. Maybe he'd been shot in the chest. Or the head. Maybe he'd been wearing a bulletproof vest. But it didn't look like it. His bodyguard must have leapt to protect him. Or maybe the person who'd launched himself at the candidate was actually the hit man. The reporter prayed. The onlookers shouted, and the white, blue, and red lights hovered like annoying visitors in the house's semidarkness. Gunshots sounded on the radio with the rumble of a passing train. Mom decided to turn on the TV and try to piece together what was happening. The gunfire sounded different on television. Neater, cleaner, like someone scattering millions of marbles across a tile floor. The candidate was still conscious when they took him to the hospital. That's what the news anchors kept repeating. Minute-by-minute coverage. Julia and my grandmother joined the reporters' prayers, calling on the saints to save his life.

I asked my mom if she knew what it felt like to have a bullet enter your body, but she didn't answer.

I went back to the window. The police cars had silenced their sirens. As my face glowed in the blinking lights, I thought about lead exploding into blood.

Bullets must feel like lots of hammer-blows on the bones. Or like endless bites from an army of ants.

After a little while, both the police cars and the crowd started to disperse.

It seemed that the man had died.

9

María wanted us to devise a plan for me to overcome my fear of going outside. She was tired of waiting for my grandfather's study door to be released from his control and eager to conquer other untamed territories.

That morning, she was bored of being stuck indoors and determined to set out for the corner store, where she wanted to buy a blackberry ice pop that came with a set of glow-in-the-dark vampire fangs as a prize. I thought her plan was risky at best, and I reminded her cruelly that she didn't have enough money for frozen treats. I suggested that we wait until my mom came back from her friend's house; then she'd take us herself and buy up all the gum, gummy candy, and chocolate cigars in the store. I invented stories about what would happen to us when we ate all those sweets: our guts would be covered in sugar and a green, tutti-frutti-flavored substance would run through our veins instead of blood. I even vowed that if she changed her mind, I'd give her any doll she wanted. But María was fed up with our captivity and hell-bent on leaving the house. Every few minutes, she drifted toward the window or sprawled in front of the front door and tried to guess what was happening on the other side. Sometimes she got so impatient that she looked like a four-legged animal, clawing at the vestibule floor, demanding fresh air. Her complaints were ignored by my grandmother and by Julia, who was too busy keeping the house clean to take us to the park. Sometimes she even made María do the dusting.

"Nothing bad is going to happen, I promise," she insisted, trying to convince me with her seductive voice.

"María, no," I answered adamantly. "I'm scared. What if they find out?"

No one's going to find out. I swear.

I continued the game, inventing new escape plans. Half-joking, half-serious, I proposed that we wear our masks. No one would recognize us with sequined, feathered faces; we could go around undetected. The worst thing that could happen would be that Julia might see us before we left the house, mistake us for my grandmother's blackbirds, and try to stick us back in the cage. In which case we'd flap our wings furiously and tear off our masks in the chaos, revealing our true identities.

Outside, we'd need María's animal powers to communicate with the wolf and ask him not to bother us as we made our way to the store. She'd use her feline telepathy to arrange when we could turn back and return home unscathed. But María thought my ideas were stupid: all we had to do was put one brave, steady foot in front of the other, she insisted, because Julia and my grandparents probably wouldn't even notice we were gone.

The door was heavy; I needed both hands to push it open. My palms, damp with nervous sweat, were instantly infused with its acidic steel-smell, and I had to rub my palms on my legs to get rid of it. The pavement was as rough as the side of a matchbox. For an instant, I thought that the friction between my patent leather shoes and the street might spark a tiny combustion and set me on fire. I took a few timid steps toward the edge of the sidewalk—the border between the house and the street—and could go no further. María, meanwhile, sauntered down the middle of the street, unconcerned about her inevitable run-in with a car. She called out to me. My legs didn't respond. My skin stiffened with vertigo. I instinctively bent over and planted my hands on the ground like pegs to support my body weight. Jeering, María doubled back and stuck her hands under my armpits. She helped me upright and took me by the arm, whispering to me not to be afraid. I let her guide me with her confident panther-steps. We passed two houses before we saw the silhouette of the wolf approaching in the distance.

I stopped dead and asked if we could go home. Her telepathic powers had failed. I felt my stomach churning into a fierce miniature hurricane that would soon swallow up my shoes, the street, the houses, the hills, María, and the wolf, and the premonition made my eyes well up with tears. María ignored my entreaties and kept walking. Nothing bad was going to happen, she repeated, and we had to hurry up. The longer we took, the madder my grandparents would be.

I had no choice but to trust her.

She put an arm around me and we walked toward the wolf. My legs trembled. I couldn't take my eyes off the sinister shadow coming into focus. Every step we took revved up the engine of my heart; my chest and ribcage hummed as if I'd swallowed a motorcycle or a beehive. The wolf walked with his head bowed, his path zigzagging and erratic. I wanted to cross to the other sidewalk, but the pressure of María's arm around my shoulders was as strong as if she were teaching me the intricate steps of a ballroom dance. She handled my body like a puppeteer. I was trapped. I took a deep breath and closed my eyes. There was no avoiding our encounter with the wolf.

One step. Another. One more and we were right in front of his enormous, bloodied, calloused feet.

I glanced up and saw his huge teeth glinting in the sun. His eyes were as gray as the pavement. I was afraid to look too far into those cloudy hollows and quickly averted my eyes.

A step.

Then nothingness.

A firm shove from María, pushing me squarely into the wolf and running away.

Like a pinball shooting out of a machine, my body pitched into his side, bounced back, and struck his legs. I lost my balance. As I tried to steady myself, I opened my arms in a gesture of submission.

If the wolf was going to grab me by the neck and take me away, I wouldn't resist.

The seconds distended.

I fell to the ground.

The wolf walked on, indifferent to my body, which was now splayed on the sidewalk, while María scampered down the block in the opposite direction, helpless with laughter.

My knees turned into volcanoes. They'd smashed against the concrete and were now releasing the ardor and the fury of molten lava. I wanted to cry, but my rage was more powerful. I imagined the house I'd built with my dad and María. I knew there was no place for her betrayal in my kingdom. I let out a yell in the middle of the street, but this time it wasn't a wail; it was a crude roar rising up from my very depths. I stood up and ran all the way to my grandparents' front door. I started to kick at it with all my strength. The booming steel clanged like the din of a thunderstorm.

María grabbed me from behind, begging me to calm down; the racket would only give away the secret of our adventure. I wrested my arms from her grip and shooed her away like a fly. I didn't want her to talk to me. I didn't want her to touch me. I didn't want to feel her breath close to me. Julia flung open the door and saw my bloody knees. She told us to hurry and come inside before my grandparents realized what was going on, and immediately started to scold María. This was the last time she'd ever bring her here, she said. Every reproach lit a spark of revenge in my eyes and encouraged me to cry, which I did, freely and with relish. Julia tried to comfort me, and so did an apprehensive María, but nothing she could do or say would cool my volcanic wrath: it had turned to magma by now, liquefied into tears that drenched my cheeks.

What on earth is all this racket, girls?

Julia tried to explain what was happening, but my grandmother cut her off, asking her to just do her job and ignore my childish whims. And she admonished Julia for letting María spend so much time at the house. If the little girl was just an excuse for Julia to neglect her duties, then it was best for her not to come at all. I interrupted my grandmother's tirade in a firm, steady voice, much like her own voice when she addressed us:

"It's okay, Grandma. I don't want María to come over anymore. I'm tired of playing with her."

10

I remember my father as an amphibious creature who fervently wanted me to inherit his love of swimming.

Dad seemed obsessed with making a champion swimmer of me, as if this were the only paternal responsibility he had to master. I, meanwhile, believed that every body of water concealed a bottomless well where I could never float. I was irremediably convinced that the pool would swallow me up, merciless as a huge, hungry toilet, much like the cosmic typhoon that was going to wash away the world. But my blind devotion to my father led me to accept his invitation without protest. We were going to a hot spring in a town near where he lived. In exchange, he promised that he'd be infinitely patient and wouldn't make me get into the water until I was ready.

It took us a couple hours to drive there. Surrounded by palm trees and banana fronds, merengue songs and "La Macarena" in the background, the pool looked like a luminous lawn grooved with syncopated waves. The scent of chlorine scraped at my skin and parched my hair with a hygienic abrasiveness that was jumbled together with the happy shouts of children playing and running around the slippery edge, untroubled by the depth of the water. Dad wasted no time getting in and asked me to stay on a lawn chair near the side of the pool so he could keep an eye on me. Alone in the sun as my father swam, I felt a pang of missing María. Several weeks had passed since the wolf incident. Like the dense fog that wreathed the highway we'd taken all the way here, my rage had finally cleared. In its place, I felt a profound longing for her raucous laughter, so different from the shrieks of these other kids that rang around the pool.

Seated in silence on the flat plastic chair, I watched suspiciously as the others gathered their courage and funneled themselves down a slide that released them into the deep end. I felt an impulse to run over and join their celebration. But my stomach turned at the thought of sliding into that viscous corpuscle. Steeped in nausea, distracted by the other kids and their commotion, I lost sight of my father.

The Jell-O had swallowed him, I thought. I was swamped with fear.

I couldn't make out a single trace of his graceful swishing reptile arms or his broad back, easily mistaken for a shark flank from this distant edge. It occurred to me that I might never see him again. I'd have to wait for Mom and my grandparents to notice our absence and come rescue me.

The skin on my whole body prickled with panic. I was going to spend the rest of my life on this chair.

I closed my eyes and clung to María's hand.

I felt myself being lifted hard from the floor. A violent force plunged me into the water. We were in it, under it, together. I felt a brief asphyxia, my head thawing. I sank my nails into his back. Then the deepest silence. The voices of the other swimmers, the children's yells, the garish tropical music—they all went quiet under the water. My body lightened. I opened my eyes. Everything was submerged in blue. I was surrounded by legs moving in slow motion; I wanted to move toward them. I shot back to the surface. I opened my mouth and received a gulp of air that swelled my lungs.

There's no reason to be scared of the water, sweetie, my father whispered. I clasped his neck, trembling, and drew my face toward the shelter of his wet body.

Dad placed one arm under my legs and another beneath my head. He asked me to lie down and close my eyes. Before I could learn to swim, I had to learn to float. We made our way all around the pool. When I was ready, he asked me to stretch out facedown, keeping my head above water. I felt safe, as if my father's arms were the perfect protection against any possible capsizing. He asked me to kick the water with my legs, and when I started to do it, he said I couldn't stop until I touched the edge of the pool or else I'd drown. I reached the finish line, exhausted, and inhaled another mouthful of air. It made my bones shudder. I sank down calmly until the soles of my feet met the tile floor and ejected me to the surface again. Dad took me in his arms and I could smell the harsh chlorine coating his skin.

That night, we sat for a long time in the car, right outside my grandparents' house, and before he choreographed my handover to Julia or my grandmother to avoid Mom, he said he had another surprise for me. He took out an old book. This is how I'd learn to read, he said. I opened it cautiously, afraid it might disintegrate in my hands, and he started to show me the vowels.

a walked with his Aunt Martha to the *park*.

e went to buy a present for *me*.

i took a shower and started to *sing*.

o saw the animals at the *zoo*.

u rode her bike all the way to *Peru*.

Then he showed me how certain letters sounded and how they were written and spelled out alongside the others. The first page illustrated a corpulent feline perched on a little rug, front paws tucked under him, smirking gently. The caption read *The fat cat sat on the mat*. I repeated it like a mantra until I'd memorized the flat sound of the *a* with its respective consonants. The next page showed a tall, mustached man dressed in white and crowned with a tall white hat; he towered over various pots and pans as they steamed on a stovetop, studying an open volume and stirring with a wooden spoon.

"The cook took a look at the book," I told my father fluently, proving that he'd initiated me into the combinatorial logic of sound.

Now I knew about echoes.

That day, he'd submerged me into the silence of the underwater world. And now, unafraid, I showed him I was capable of perceiving the sounds that lived inside the alphabet.

My father praised me with a damp kiss and I threw my arms around his neck. I wanted to tell him everything that had been happening behind the front doors of my grandparents' house. I wanted to start from the beginning. My mother and her absence, my grandmother and her distance, María and her betrayal. The beast. Its howling, its temper, how it rattled my bones whenever I got anywhere near its forbidden closet.

When he said it was time to get out of the car, I looked him in the eye and gathered my nerve to tell him about all the houses I'd imagined living in with him. My most fervent wish was for the two of us to go far, far away, to a desert where we'd ride wild camels and live on rice and eggs, and where I'd never have to worry about my grandmother's fury or the sorrow I felt on the tip of my tongue every time I thought about María. But the words didn't come out as I'd hoped.

"I don't want to live in this house anymore," I confessed. "I want to be with you."

I felt, for an instant, that my body had gone utterly light.

He stared at me. He looked surprised. He took my face into his tortoiseshell hands and planted kisses on my eyelids.

I pressed myself into his neck and told him how much I loved him. He looked at me gently and drew his lips close to my ear.

"I promise I'll talk with your mom about all this. I'd like us to spend more time together, too."

We said goodbye with a handshake, as if we were finalizing an important business deal, and as I walked into the house, my heart felt as big as a hot-air balloon. I climbed the stairs, trying to remember the shape of the vowels.

a, a grain of salt.

e, a cat taking a nap.

i, a streetlamp.

o, a headless snail.

u, a cow's thick blue tongue.

a, a drop of vinegar.

e, a slippery staircase.

i, a bleeding cut.

o, my mother's lips.

u, the language of the ambulances outside my house.

11

The afternoons were long and heavy without María. I tried to re-create our games, but they just felt like lifeless simulations of offices, supermarkets, and schools. Whenever I had an idea for a new adventure or made a joke, all I received in return was the cold, indifferent gaze of my dolls and stuffed animals, and I gave up. Television had started to bore me, too. I killed a lot of time in my bedroom, studying the reading book my father had given me. I quickly progressed from ants and alligators to ferrets and fireflies, and then to icicles and iguanas and koalas and kangaroos, until I finally reached the page about a large, gray, humpbacked bird, the *ñandú* in Spanish, which fixed its hollow, slightly cross-eyed stare on its friend the *ñu*, a kind of spindly bull with zebra skin sketched between its ribs. I could spend hours and hours tracing the silhouettes of these mysterious animals with my fingertips. I tried to pronounce their names, feeling out the *ñ*, letting it reverberate all the way into the point of my nose, flaring my nostrils until I couldn't sustain the grimace any longer. But these linguistic pastimes didn't hold a candle to the pleasure I'd found with María and her songs, and I missed her more and more.

That morning, like a perfectly synchronized coincidence, I picked up the phone and heard my father on the line. I didn't recognize him at first, because his voice didn't sound as deep and warm as when he whispered strange animal facts into my ear. He seemed nervous, and the timbre of his voice was sharper, maybe because the connection distorted it; he stammered a bit. It wasn't the same sound I associated with his lavish black hair—a thick, steady buzz I wanted to sink my fingers into.

Before I could say hello, I realized my mother was also on the phone. She sounded different, too. Her sweet, tender tone had gone chilly and tight, and her voice had a caustic edge like my grandmother's.

Dad asked Mom if he could spend more time with me. But his voice quavered and he paused several times between words like the pulsing of a telegraph. On the other end, Mom responded with a single syllable, sharp and final: *No.*

Dad, exasperated, began to rattle off his rights. He argued that we enjoyed our time together and I myself had made this request of him. My heart beat faster to hear him talk about me. My father was the hero who had finally vowed to rescue me from the razor-sharp talons of the beast. He would whisk me away to the house I'd always dreamed of. But my mother only replied with a series of curt refusals. She told him off, invoked old fights they'd had when they were together. Her rough responses to my father's questions made me think of hundreds of fish heads set out in the sun to dry. The reek of them.

Their relationship was completely unimaginable to me: I'd never even seen them in the same room. I struggled to believe that they'd ever shared the same space, the same breath, before I existed. At that point, no fantasy or game could make me understand that the only living, breathing, sweating, salivating indicator, the only three-dimensional evidence of that chance encounter between two strangers who had little or nothing in common, was me.

My father's voice was a timorous rattle begging to be heard. My mother's voice, though, was getting shriller by the minute, and she interrupted him with accusations. My father talked about responsibility, stability, and care. My mother growled that no one would ever take her daughter away from her and she'd hire a lawyer if she had to. My father ignored her threats and kept pleading for a little more time with me. I blushed when I thought of us sleeping in the same bed. We'd make a life together. I'd show him all the progress I was making in the book he'd given me. He'd never abandon me again. But their shouts jolted me out of my daydream and left me stunned by their insults, which swelled like the tide when the moon is full.

Suddenly, as my mother was midway through another tirade against my father, he must have thrown the phone to the ground. Jarred by the staticky interference shrieking over the line, blaring across the chasm between my parents, I flared my nose to get some air. I suddenly felt like I'd stuck my tongue into a sea of salt and sour milk. My palms sweated. A pale, viscous substance coursed through my entire body and churned my stomach. I let go of the phone and lay down on the tile floor to soothe the sickly heat rising up in me. Fixing my eyes on the ceiling, I started to prod the edge of my teeth with my tongue until I found one that was loose. I made it dance against my gum to distract myself from what I'd overheard. The conversation was still ricocheting inside the walls of my mind.

I made my index finger and thumb into a set of pincers and yanked out the tooth.

I clutched it in my left fist and savored the blood pooling into my mouth. That's what raw ox meat must taste like. I licked my right palm. I saw with my own eyes that the liquid swimming around inside me was still as red as it had always been.

12

Those were the nightmare days.

I climbed a spiral staircase to the very top of a tower, where my father was waiting. There were so many steps and they were so far apart that my legs felt heavy, my body sapped of strength as I went up. When I thought I'd finally reached the end of the stairs, I realized that I'd have to climb even higher if I was going to reach my father. Then I was standing in the middle of an infinite corridor and saw Dad on the other side. He hadn't yet noticed I was there. I started running toward him. Suddenly I saw a shadow open a tiny door—the shadow might have been my mother—and a violent rush of water surged in. The current rose and swept away everything in its path: paintings, tables, couches, chandeliers. The unstoppable river came closer and closer to me, and I tried to run to the other side, to my father. But my legs cleaved to the ground like iron pegs and I couldn't move them.

I woke drenched in sweat, my heart lurching and swerving so hard that it threatened to leave my chest. My screams woke Mom and she sat down beside me on the bed and placed her hands on my back, waiting for my heartbeat to slow. Sometimes she touched my forehead and cheeks, worried that my fever wasn't dropping. She lifted me out of bed and gave me a long bath; I shook with cold spasms from head to toe and my skin crawled with goose bumps. The only thing that soothed the chill I felt inside me was a long drink of sticky pink syrup that was supposed to cure all manner of children's ailments.

The vinegary aftertaste on the back of my throat became a thin, hot slime I swallowed over and over, trying to force it down my esophagus and into my stomach, where it would spread through the rest of my body and start to warm me up again. The days were very short and I mistook my dreams for wakefulness. Sometimes, when I wanted to walk to Julia's room or the kitchen, my legs felt as heavy as two rusty anchors, and the mere thought of being immobilized when the great wave flooded the house sent me straight back to bed, trembling with fear.

On one of those afternoons, Mom woke me up with gentle kisses on my eyelids. She asked me to come with her to the kitchen because she wanted to make a special dinner for my grandparents and for me. She had some very good news. We spent the rest of the day among pots of boiling water and pasta sauce. I helped her grate the cheese with the fastidiousness and care of an antique porcelain restorer. Julia beat egg whites with such force that they became a dense white foam and stayed perfectly still, as if by magic, even when she turned the bowl upside-down over her head. Mom sang bits of the Spanish-language ballads that came on the radio, and she sometimes asked us to turn up the volume, especially when Luis Miguel's songs appeared among the Top 40. My mother's good mood wafted together with the warm scent of cheese melting in the oven and the herbs seasoning the meat. I felt overcome with a new kind of appetite, eager to eat anything I could find in the pantry and the fridge.

My insatiable hunger scared off the fever.

The only one who seemed irritated with the festivities was my grandfather. He didn't see the point of all the paraphernalia, all the cloth napkins and bone china for an ordinary dinner. But Mom, as a preventative measure, asked Julia to keep his glass full of red wine so he'd drink away his annoyance. This was a special occasion, and she wasn't going to let his foul temper ruin her announcement.

By the time my grandparents and my mother had gotten up from the dinner table and moved to the living room to keep drinking, I felt well enough to scamper all over the house again. I was even inspired to improvise a game of hopscotch on the kitchen floor. I remembered how María had taught me to play, and I replaced the areas assigned to "heaven" and "hell" with "forest" and "catastrophe." I was very restless, and as the others chatted about the weather and the news, I settled under the coffee table to play carousel and stables in peace. My fingers were horses leaping tirelessly around the table legs. I wanted to turn into those horses, to gallop around every room in the house.

"I got a job," I heard Mom say above the table. "And that's not all. I got a very good job."

My mother's voice lit up, shining with her good news, but my grandmother brushed her off. She couldn't believe that my mother could get a prestigious job, much less keep it. But Mom persisted excitedly, describing her new responsibilities, her enormous office. My grandmother, curt, only wanted to know who'd helped her pull it off, and Mom launched into a litany of praise for someone named Álvaro, a friend of my grandparents who had always seemed interested in my mother. The low hum of adult conversation melted into the whinnying of the horses as they cantered through my mind.

There was a sudden change of subject and my mother's earnestness shrank into hesitation. She told my grandparents that she'd seen Álvaro a couple of weeks earlier and he'd offered her the job. She also said that they were dating. With these words, she lowered her shoulders and her head as if awaiting a blow from my grandfather. A scolding. A reproach. But at the other end of the living room, the beast smiled, satisfied, and spat something about how lucky she was to have snagged a good man, one who was willing to accept her with a spoiled brat in tow. Startled by his reaction, Mom didn't protest. She suggested a toast. Their glasses clinked as I tried to pacify one of my horses, offering him sugar cubes and bread crumbs. It occurred to me that I'd have to break him quickly: now, more than ever, I'd need a trusty quadruped to carry me all the way to the house I was going to build with my father.

My grandfather was happy. We were only halfway through the year, but he started singing Christmas songs, and his words diluted and liquefied in his mouth, every syllable soaked in a swamp of liquor. He even asked my grandmother to dance. She laughed and let herself be lurched along by the brusque movements of the beast.

Mom took advantage of the general euphoria to propose a way they could celebrate this turn of fortune. It would be my birthday soon, and she wanted to throw a big party. They'd invite all the family friends, their children, grandchildren, nieces, nephews. *Viva!* my grandfather crowed, and took a great swig of alcohol. He called for another toast and released my grandmother from his grip. The beast took a well-aimed swipe and hooked me around the back. He wanted to make me sit in his lap, but I was smarter. Hot phlegm wriggled out like a worm from the back of my throat to the tip of my tongue. I spat onto his feet. Before he could say a thing, I made a break for my room, where I distracted myself with the reading book. I could hear the strains of my mother's and grandparents' drunken laughter. There they would stay, carousing in the living room, until the wee hours of the morning.

I climbed into bed and got ready to go to sleep. Mom came in to say goodnight and sat on the quilt. I lay across her lap; she stroked my hair and asked if I was still feverish. She checked my temperature. Confirming my recovery, she asked about María and why she hadn't come back to play. Without going into details, I told her we'd fought, and she promised she'd help me convince Julia to bring her back. She'd be the guest of honor at my party, and we could play together and meet the other kids who would bring me lots of presents.

I drifted slowly into sleep as Mom described the pale fur of the rabbits a magician would pull out of a hat. Just for me.

II

1

A tickle crept up my legs and made it impossible for me to keep still. The anxious twitch erupted so violently that it shook the silverware laid out on the dining room table and my grandmother shot me one of her icy glares. But I couldn't help it. My heart was a pressure cooker about to burst. My stomach teemed with hundreds of stampeding antelopes, and my insides galloped with anticipation.

I was about to see María for the first time in months.

I was restless. I wasn't sure if she wanted to see me, too, or if Julia had forced her to come. I imagined the countless things we'd do together. But then I had the wrenching thought that my games might not interest her anymore, and a cold sweat prickled my palms. I even thought about going outside, if she asked me to; I wanted to make her happy no matter what. Even if it meant stepping onto the wolf's bloody feet and traveling the streets with his sack of glass shards.

As I sank deeper into all the possible ways our reunion might go, sheathed in dread like a diving suit made of rusty metal and worst-case scenarios, I suddenly felt María's damp breath on my neck. My whole body flinched with surprise, and when I turned around, I found myself facing her open arms, ready to clasp me in a stiff hug. I rested my head near her ear and took a sniff of her hair. It smelled sweet, fruity. She patted me twice on the back: two paperweights. Everything that happened on the day of her betrayal returned to me like a blaze of lightning. The weight of her hands—the same hands that had shoved me onto the pavement—was instantly unbearable.

María needed to understand that I wasn't the weak little girl she once knew. Now I was Inés, brave animal. I'd lost three more teeth and I could touch the bottom of the pool and hold my breath for ten seconds. I could also read all the signs at the drugstores, corner stores, and cafeterias along the blocks that separated my grandparents' house from the park, while María could barely write her own name.

I was Inés, demon. Inés, submarine. Inés, half-falcon, half-hammerhead shark.

I shook off María's hug and grabbed her arm. If we were going to play together, I was the one who'd get to make the rules. Any act of disobedience on her part would make me tattle to Julia and my grandmother and she'd be banished once more. First, I wanted to force my friend to listen nonstop to "La Lambada," which I was proud to own on tape. One of my TV shows constantly replayed a video of two kids dancing in the middle of a group of grown-ups, and I'd learned the steps by heart. I pressed Play. With the first accordion chords, introducing the mournful voice of a woman singing in Portuguese, I placed my hand on María's back and started moving my hips, guiding her feet as she tried to follow the rhythm. I'd practiced in front of the mirror a few times, hoping I'd get to dance like this with my father someday. But now, with María, I had the perfect opportunity to rehearse the steps I'd show my dad when we moved away to a place like the one in the video: a barge in the middle of the jungle, where the river would be the only witness to our new lives.

We danced the song over and over until we learned the sequence of steps, and María suggested we put on a show in the living room with my mother as the audience. I explained that my mother had been staying at Álvaro's house for a whole long week—planning my birthday party, she said when she called me every night before bed. And now that I was the queen of the blackbirds, no one was going to clip my wings: I could fly unfettered all over my grandparents' house.

María rehearsed my choreography in a feverish trance. Taking advantage of her distraction, I scurried off to the bathroom. Halfway between my bedroom and the end of the hall, a glimmer of light slipped in through the crack under a door and hovered on the tiles, stopping me in my tracks. I blinked hard to focus on the image before me. I stood very still in front of the door to my grandfather's studio and stared.

Someone had left it open.

I ran back to my room and seized María's hand. I liked feeling that our roles had switched: now she was the one who didn't have a chance to breathe, the one who had no idea where I was pulling her so earnestly. We stopped at the door. I gave her a push before she could say a word. Together, we walked into the territory that had been off-limits to us for so long.

"Inés, there's nothing here," María said, disappointed. "And everything smells like old people."

María's words were a faint, faraway gurgle, so remote that they couldn't possibly distract me from the mission I had to fulfill inside that mysterious room.

Let's get out of here before they catch us.

I started to rummage through every drawer in the huge oak desk, searching for the treasures that María's eyes were unable to detect. Memo pads, perfumed sheets of paper, erasers of all sizes—perfect for fattening our coffers of forgotten loot. Amid all the objects I snatched up greedily and handed over to María so she could stuff them into her pockets, I saw the talisman, the object of my fantasies during all those hours I'd spent lying under the desk and playing ballerina: the key to my grandfather's closet.

Out of the blue, I was faced with the possibility of opening the lock to the most top-secret place in the whole house. Drunk with excitement, desperate to solve the mystery at last, I picked up the key and tried impatiently to jam it into the mechanism. I suspected I was about to uncover a treasure trove that would turn María green with envy—and I wasn't going to share it with her. I had to jiggle the key several times before it turned. On the other side of the door, right next to the safe, I found myself staring at the strangest object I'd ever seen.

Dark

Erect.

Tense.

Radiant as the silence of the ocean's nocturnal depths.

My grandfather's hunting rifle.

A seductive, hypnotic voice slipped out of the barrel and overpowered me. Softly, it commanded me to pick up the gun and caress it. To touch the trigger, press it. To bring the tip of my tongue to the rifle's mouth and savor the particles of dust. To decipher, all by myself, the residual echoes after the roar of a shot. The murmur of catastrophe. The hum that would accompany the end of the world.

We didn't hear my grandparents coming home. We didn't hear my grandmother shouting for me to help her carry the groceries inside or my grandfather's footsteps approaching the study. When he found us, I was inside the closet, meticulously studying the rifle. He lashed out a paw, plucked me out, and slammed the door. He threw me to the ground and roared. He didn't understand what I was doing in there when I'd been strictly forbidden to be anywhere near his things. I covered my head to shield myself from his punches. When he turned around, I rose nimbly to my feet and launched myself at him, sinking my teeth into his leg. Both my new incisors and my old fangs formed ruthless little daggers and wounded the beast. He grabbed me by the head and shoved me out of the study, bellowing all the while.

He would change the locks or shut me up in my room forever, with no birthday parties and no visits from my father. He'd do anything to keep me away from what was none of my business, from where I wasn't welcome.

2

The night we had leg of lamb for dinner was the night Mom came home after spending a week at Álvaro's house. I remember because I didn't like the woody, bloody taste of the lamb and I devised a strategy to clear my plate. First I chewed the meat until it softened and then I removed it from my mouth in discreet little balls, hiding them in my napkin or tossing them onto the floor undetected. Or at least that's what I thought.

"Inés, please, stop doing that," my grandmother said firmly. "You're making us all uncomfortable."

I responded with an indifferent glance and continued to squeeze my meat into tiny lumps.

Inés, please.

I can still see my mother walking barefoot into the dining room, holding her shoes in one hand, her hair pulled back with a pen that pierced the thick skeins of her curls and clutched them in an indecipherable tangle.

She crossed the doorway and a silent curtain lifted over our heads.

My grandfather began to take deep sips of whiskey. My grandmother couldn't look my mother in the eye. They ate wordlessly, separating the meat from the bone before swallowing large mouthfuls of its red pulp. My grandmother broke the hush with some remark about my mother's appearance, her voice breathy with scorn. She didn't even bother to glare at her. She kept asking me to stop playing with my food, more emphatic every time.

The screech of the knife against the plate and the ice

cubes clinking against my grandfather's glass formed what sounded like a carefully orchestrated dissonance. Julia approached warily and served another slice of meat to my grandfather, who was never full.

Mom ventured several topics of conversation in hopes of breaking the silence. She said something about a Japanese woman who spent forty hours locked in an elevator, but no one took the bait. She tried to win over my grandfather by chatting about soccer and asking how his team had fared in the Libertadores final, but he simply went on eating as if he hadn't heard her.

Every single word my mother clumsily volunteered was met with monosyllables, and the silence grew denser and denser until it had engulfed the dinner table like a thick fog.

"Inés! That's enough!" My grandfather's fist slammed down on the table, interrupting the fleshy clicks of teeth and spit. "When will you get it through your head that food is meant to be eaten, not manhandled?"

Mom softly came to my defense, but my grandfather barked at her, too. She'd forgotten me, he spat, and now I was more unruly than ever. I'd been digging around in his things again. I'd even bitten him. The girl was out of control without a mother to teach her how to behave. And Mom was shameless, spreading her legs for the boss after two days on the job. He took shots at her desire to live a footloose life, unencumbered by responsibilities or children. At how men drove her crazy. At how my father had driven her crazy and then she'd dated an army of idiots. About how we'd never respected his house.

Mom struggled to keep her composure under his barrage of accusations, tried to explain what was happening. She was just spending time with her boyfriend. She wanted to build a different life with him than the one she was used to. She didn't feel that she had to ask permission or make excuses to her father for what was going on, but she was making an effort to talk with him anyway, to thank him for everything he'd done for us. He interrupted the speech she was carefully trying to assemble. And his words shook the walls of the house:

"Shut up, you stupid whore."

My mother's face went bright. She seized her cutlery and her eyes filled with tears of rage as my grandfather loomed over her.

She rose from the table and stood before him. Impulsively, she grabbed the end of the tablecloth and yanked it hard.

Broken plates.

Shouts and broken plates.

"What are you going to do? Are you going to hit me?" my mother screamed, defiant. "Do it, sir. That's the only way you think problems can be solved. I'm not afraid of you."

Hit me.

And with a swift, vigorous sweep of his hand, my grandfather grabbed her by the hair and forced her onto her knees on the dining room floor. His hands trembled uncontrollably, his belt buckle chattering like a set of teeth in cold air as he struggled to unfasten it. When he finally managed to free the strap from his belt loops, he gripped it like a whip.

He looked my mother in the eye. Something changed in him then, as if her eyes called him back from the brink—from the feral urge to attack his own child. He spat onto the floor beside her. Then he left the room without another word.

I spent the entire scene sitting mutely in front of my grandmother, kneading the little balls of meat I didn't want to swallow. I looked at my mother, now sprawled facedown on the floor. Her back rose gently with every breath like a dry leaf in the breeze. She lifted her head and I tried to send her a caring look, but she couldn't see me.

Her eyes were blinded by mascara and tears.

3

It's just for a few days. It'll just be for a few days, I promise.
We'll come back to celebrate your birthday. A close-up of
my mother's mouth. The tiny cracks on her lips filmed
with fuchsia, the color moving in a slow smear as she
repeated her words like a mantra. Her mouth looked
swollen from this distance. As if she'd spent last night
staving off a flock of woodpeckers. Or as if dense spi-
derwebs had sprouted from her lips and she'd had to rip
them out with her teeth. I remember my mother's mouth.
Very close. Salivating, repeating promises I didn't see
why she had to make, flurrying my cheeks with kisses.
Her mouth in slow motion, her body shifting all over the
room. From one wall to the other. Tireless. Sketching
invisible lines in all directions as she packed my suitcase.

I looked at it spread slack-jawed on the mattress. I
tried to guess where we were going, judging only by the
objects my mother struggled to cram inside.

Bathing suit: we were definitely going to the beach.
I imagined myself beside her, the two of us supine on
the sand, waiting for the dolphins to come and prod us
gently into the water, like when María and I played mer-
maids in the bathtub.

Rubber boots: we wouldn't need shoes at the bottom
of the ocean. So we were going hiking in the mountains
to see what the deer were up to. Once we reached the
summit, we'd be able to see all the cities in the world
from way up high and we'd decide which one we felt like
parachuting down into.

Gloves and scarf: the air would be very cold when we were in free fall, which is why we'd need to cover our mouths and ears.

Flip-flops: or maybe the air would be very hot, and our shoes would melt as we made our way down to earth.

Just a few days, okay? She kept repeating it. She sat down on top of the suitcase and tried to force the zipper-teeth into a proper bite. *Promise me you'll be very good.*

"What about your suitcase, Mom?" I asked, hoping to speed up her preparations and finally set off for wherever we were headed.

"Sweetie, I'm not going with you."

Something in my eyes must have unsettled her, because she threw her arms around me, stroked my hair, and kissed the top of my head.

She explained, gently, that I'd be spending a few days at my father's house. I felt like my heart was going to leap out of my chest. I thought we'd be traveling together, all three of us, and for a few seconds I let myself be enticed by the idea of having a family. But she quickly clarified that only I was leaving: it was the first time we'd ever be apart. Only I would go live with my dad for a little while, until she figured things out at my grandparents' house. I wanted to ask Mom if I could bring María, so I could make the home I'd always wanted. But before I could shape the words, I saw that my mother was weeping mutely. Her tears felt far more catastrophic than any storm that threatened to bury the cosmos.

Now I remember this scene and I see myself as a private eye, an intimate sleuth trying to solve some of the enigmas that my mother's silence eventually concealed altogether. In those moments, when I try to fill the gaps in my own memory, I understand that this was when my mother decided to start a new life with Álvaro. She needed some time away from me so she could pull herself together and leave—finally—my grandparents' supervision. Maybe that's why I sensed a glimmer of relief in her eyes, even in the middle of all the guilt. It would be a painful separation, but also a necessary one. We couldn't languish in that brutal habitat any longer.

Mom turned around and wheeled the suitcase out of the room, still repeating *it's just for a few days it's just for a few days.* Julia came upstairs to let her know that my dad was waiting outside. Mom gave me another kiss or two on the top of my head, and I said a telepathic goodbye to each and every one of my toys. I was going to my father's house, and even though she said it was just for a little while, I knew he'd ask me to stay forever once we'd spent all those nights together in the country. I made my way down the spiral staircase, step by step, saying goodbye, goodbye to every corner of the house I'd conquered with María. And just before Julia shut the heavy iron front door, *bam!*, my ghost-double appeared in the doorway to say goodbye, too.

She lifted her hand, shyly, her eyes soft, and she waved at me.

I mirrored her gesture and told her to be good.

4

Dad lived a couple of hours outside the city, in the middle of the countryside. To get to his cabin, we had to skirt the hills along a narrow highway and delve deep into a dense, cold forest that smelled of eucalyptus seeds and soil after a downpour.

There's a word for this smell, just like there's a word for almost everything.

I remember his sweet voice as he took my hand and walked at my pace down the path connecting the car to the front door of the house. It was like treading a loose carpet with bits of pine needles for threads. They stuck to my shoes like slender coppery worms.

"Petrichor. That's the word for the smell of rain in dry places. Pe. Tri. Chor."

And when he pronounced the *r*'s, they made a cluster of gurgling sounds that tangled in his throat.

"Open your mouth," he instructed me. "Open wide. There, all the way in the back—have you ever seen that little dangly thing that makes you want to hit it like a punching bag?"

And as he said this, he brought his fists close to my face like a boxer and feigned a blow. When I blinked reflexively and yanked my head back, he took my face into his open palms and gave me a kiss on the cheek.

"That's the uvula. There's a word for almost everything. Do you know what this is called?"

And he gently rubbed the space between my nose and my upper lip.

"Mustache," I said arrogantly.

"No, pretty girl," he laughed, his voice sweet as a jet of honey. "Medial cleft. Or philtrum. And this space between your teeth?" He stuck a long finger into my mouth and poked me right at the edge of the gum where a new tooth was budding.

The soft touch of his hands made me forget my answer, if I even had one.

I felt my spit swirling in my mouth like a wild brook and I couldn't keep from biting him. My father laughed and laughed and grabbed me around the waist, hoisting me off the ground and spinning me over his head before he set me down on his shoulders and broke into a run toward the house.

The clamor of laughter and words intensified when Sup, Dad's German shepherd, started to bark. This dog had been his only roommate for as long as he'd lived in the country. High up on my father's shoulders, I saw the animal trotting eagerly toward us. He wagged his tail, and when he reached us, he sniffed at my father's hands and leapt as high as his chest, where my legs dangled.

My first instinct was to tense up like a violin string about to snap. I'd never been so close to an animal before, and although Dad patted my knees to show me that everything was all right, it made me nervous to feel Sup panting sourly so close to my skin. Dad crooned and opened his palms to the dog's snout. Sup licked them and advanced alongside us, zigzagging between my father's feet. Dad tried to keep his balance while dodging the animal and keeping me firmly rooted up above.

When we reached the door, he lowered me to the ground and fished out his keys. As he opened it, the dog brought his wet nose to my torso and sniffed at me. I held out my hands, imitating my father's gesture moments before, and I felt little jolts of electricity up and down my arms with Sup's earnest licks.

I closed my eyes. Red and blue stains appeared behind my eyelids, changing shape with the streaks of the warm animal tongue on my skin.

Now I know there's a word for those stains. They're called phosphenes.

5

My father was a nocturnal animal. During the time I spent in his house, I learned to adapt to his strange routines, his personal time zone.

I always woke very early and waited patiently until a noise on the other side of the wall told me he was up. But the only thing I heard for most of the morning was a silence as thick as the concrete barrier between our rooms. As my hunger grew, I wriggled around in bed like a cockroach on its back. When I couldn't take the gnawing in my stomach anymore, I ventured into the kitchen in search of something to eat. My father's pantry was crammed with cans, preserves, and wine bottles, so these expeditions were usually fruitless; I ended up going back to bed and trying to sleep a little more until he woke. It took Dad a couple of days to realize what was going on. After that, he gradually stocked his shelves with Cocoa Krispies, bananas, and milk I could serve myself while he slept.

I woke him by midmorning, prying open his right eyelid to lick his eyeball. The tip of my tongue slipped easily over the viscous surface of his eye and traced a perfect parabola. The sweet taste led me to conclude that my father's tears were made of river-water and the dark pupil I'd inherited from him was none other than a huge, striped fish darting across the surface. Dad smiled and wrinkled his nose as he tried to shake his head hard enough to shoo me off. Then he grabbed me and pulled me into bed, where we played and talked until lunch.

Dad liked silence. He said it was what he needed most for his work. Every afternoon, he brought me to his room, turned on the Betamax, and played an animated movie about a little boy who lived in the jungle with a bear and a panther. The boy wanted to be a wild animal like his friends, but they knew it was best for him to rejoin his species. When an orangutan appeared and sang a snappy song, I stood up on the bed and jumped to the beat. Working at the dining room table that served as his office, Dad shut the door against the noise. Sometimes I emerged from the room because I wanted a glass of milk or a hug; he usually responded with a long *shhhhhhh*. He needed silence so he could write a very important essay about anatomy and literature that might earn him a scholarship to study in the United States. Whenever I tried to get his attention by reciting entire passages from the movie or parading around the living room dressed as a wild girl—I tied one of his neckties around my head and wore his sneakers on my hands like claws—he begged me not to interrupt him. The quieter I was, he vowed, the closer we'd be to moving away together.

He rattled off a few sentences, promised to take me to Disneyland, things like that. And then he returned to his labors—knocking over stacks of papers, rereading passages from books and dictionaries—and waved me back into his room. I obeyed, but only in part, because I often hid behind the wall to watch him work. He was like the monkey king from my movie, which made me laugh. He scratched his head restlessly at his typewriter, as if awaiting the arrival of words that were late for an appointment. When they appeared, his fingers jolted frenetically over the stiff keys.

I wanted to talk to my father all the time. To tell him all

the stories, to share all the information about the end of the cosmos I'd once memorized for him, to spend hours lying in the grass and reading. But whenever I came up to him, he just asked me to be quiet or to go take a nap. Maybe it was this imposition of silence that made country days feel so much longer than city days. I got very bored when he worked. By the third or fourth day, the jungle movie had faded into a predictable ambient hum that no longer excited or surprised me. I started making up games to distract myself. I imagined that María was with me, helping me hatch ways to fight monotony in the middle of nowhere: the escape game, for instance, in which we scampered out of the house, through my father's bedroom window, without him noticing. There was a large expanse of grass and trees behind the house and I liked to lie down on the green ground and dig in my nails until they came out blackened. I brought them to my mouth and savored the iodine taste of the earth. Maybe one of the games I played with María would come to life: maybe the grass would turn into a magic carpet and rise into the air and whisk me away to visit my mother.

Sometimes Sup came over and pressed his cold nose into my cheek. I felt his warm breath, the sweep of his damp tongue over my hair, as if my head were an envelope he had to lick. I took his nose in my hands and made him nod, or I lifted the corners of his mouth for a closer look at his sharp fangs. Then I rolled down the hill until I reached the barbed-wire fence that marked the limit of my father's land, and Sup came with me, darting and howling. I climbed quickly to my feet, still dizzy, and walked back up to the backyard, where I began my gymnastics routine all over again, accompanied by my four-legged squire and my conjured friend.

I challenged María and Sup to climb one of the scrawny alcaparro trees that ringed the property, but their arms and legs weren't strong enough. So I ran and leapt around the tree in an attempt to improve my stamina, hoping I'd someday make it all the way to the top. Sometimes I walked the path between the house and the front gate and collected eucalyptus seeds. I lifted them to my face and felt their tang rise into the darkness of my nose, invading it with acrid warmth. Then I rubbed them between my fingers in front of the dog's snout, awaited his opinion on the smell, and asked María if she thought the perfume was elegant. Met with canine indifference and a silent friend, I made the front of my sweater into a kind of basket and gathered the seeds like precious jewels a pirate had left behind. Finally, I slipped back into the house through my father's window without him noticing that all my clothes were covered in grass and dry leaves. When I returned to the kitchen once again in search of a snack, like a carrot or a cube of cheese, then retreated to the bedroom, I could hear my father grumbling to himself, baffled at how his impeccable floor kept filling up with forest grit.

I also liked to play invisible woman with María. We ducked under the furniture and between the curtains in the den until we reached my father's worktable and snuck up on him from behind. The first few times I tried this trick, Dad laughed and swore he didn't see how I could have surprised him without making a sound. But after repeated efforts to show off my cleverness and stealth, his patience flagged. When I tried to vary the game by stealing one of his pens and pressing down on all the keys of his keyboard with the palm of my hand, he growled and bared his teeth.

Dad, the great white shark, frightened me.

My instinct was to run back into the bedroom and hide under the covers. I panted in the darkness and felt my lungs pulsing with fear. He came into the room, pulled back the blanket, and gave me a kiss on the forehead.

"I'm sorry," he said, contrite. "I didn't mean to scare you like that. But you have to understand that those games make me really mad." He spoke slowly. "I need you to be quiet in this room and I need you not to come out until I finish working."

I don't love you when you're naughty.

His words echoed around the bedroom walls with a force I found so unbearable that I could only pull the blankets over my head again, cover my ears with my hands, and imagine that I was a fish, startled, hiding at the bottom of an aquarium.

6

I remember I felt the tingling first.

Then a blaze. My bones burning inside.

And then the pressure of two dense slabs I couldn't shake off.

Mangling me.

Crushing my tissues.

Grinding me into dust.

As if I were right at the center of the earth, between two tectonic plates shifting closer and closer, about to smash me flat. As if I were witnessing the irremediable arrival of the apocalypse.

I grabbed María's hand and squeezed it hard and let myself be overtaken by the fierceness of the pain invading my arm. Then a warm jet of urine trickled down my legs, which distracted me from the throbbing for a moment. I fell to the ground and tried to take a big gulp of air for solace. María kept quiet beside me. Her silence was soothing.

It was only when he found me that the pain momentarily stopped.

I closed my eyes and heard a dry click, like a pithy pair of castanets.

Relief.

My lungs freed from suffocation, from the full weight of my screams tearing at my sternum.

And the animal's timid yelps, sharp wails fading as the seconds passed.

I lay on my side and watched him.

My father kicked him, enraged. The animal's eyes widened with every thump. His half-smile stayed in place, even as the insults escalated. The final kick landed close to the ears. I heard a tiny water bubble pop. Nobly, he stretched out his hind legs and neck, ready to receive another blow. Dad sobbed. Sup trembled. He still had a little shred of my sweatshirt sleeve between his teeth. I shook, too. Not with the pain—my arm was completely numb—but because my pants were soaked in pee and I felt the frigid savannah wind on my legs.

Dad gathered me into his arms and carried me like a swooning bride on her wedding night. We got into the car and he drove fast. He was in such a hurry that he didn't even bother to turn on the radio and find some music for us. The last thing I remember, before I fell into a deep sleep, was resting my head on my father's lap and starting to count how many times he stepped on the pedals and changed gears. I imagined that he was the pilot of a space machine and I felt him carrying me all the way up to the summit of the sky.

7

I woke to the sound of my mother's voice: she was singing a song about wanting to know what love is. I felt her hands stroking my cheeks, and the gentle warmth distracted me briefly from the searing pain in my arm. Seated very close to her, in my grandparents' living room, was my father with a coffee mug.

My grandmother's caustic voice dissolved into the clink of the sugar cubes in my mother's cup of coffee. My grandmother addressed Dad alone, offering affectedly breezy advice, lecturing him on the risks of keeping such a large animal in the house. My father sat in silence, shielded by a stiff, awkward smile. He was incapable of speaking directly to my grandmother, but he tried; Mom jumped to his defense. Each of my grandmother's bitter comments was neutralized by my mother praising my father, trying to justify what had happened in the countryside. Dad responded kindly, but my grandmother kept cutting in to insult him, seizing every possible opportunity to condemn his negligence of me, my mother, and everything he was ever supposed to take care of. Mom sang as if she couldn't hear my grandmother at all, and Dad, sweaty-palmed, apologized repeatedly and fumbled to thank them for raising me so well. I'd been very brave and I deserved the enormous birthday party they were planning in my honor.

Mom thanked him for his words, smiling, and reached out to wipe a pastry crumb from his cheek. When she touched his face, Dad's shoulders shifted forward and his chest curved inward. Then she started in on how good a job he'd done, how swiftly he'd reacted to the emergency. The dog bite had been just a scare, and now everyone was showering me with kisses and affection.

But my grandmother clung to her hostility and insulted my father with growing fervor. He went paler with every affront, and he kept glancing toward my grandfather's study in hopes that the beast wouldn't come out—the beast was one of his greatest fears. Dad decided to make his exit while he still could and said a nervous goodbye to my mother and grandmother. He rose from the couch and I sat upright to throw my arms around his neck and beg him not to go. But before I had the chance, Mom reached out an arm and touched my father close to his hip, a gesture that brought him to a halt. She whispered something into his ear and coldly asked my grandmother to leave.

The old lady got to her feet and stalked out, wrinkling her nose as if fleeing a toxic smell.

We were left alone. It was the first time I'd ever seen my parents together with no one else in the room.

They were quiet for a while. Occasionally they laughed or exchanged glances when one brushed against the other's hand by accident as they reached for the cookie plate or the water pitcher in the middle of the table. I liked seeing them this way, enjoying each other's company. I felt my lungs and stomach surge. It was as if I had a pond full of restless fish for organs. Their laughter made me smile, and I couldn't stop thinking about the families of lions I saw on TV, going out to hunt zebras as a group.

I didn't need María anymore. My herd was complete.

8

Mom saw that I was starting to doze off and asked me to go up to bed. I protested—I wanted to spend a little more time with them—but Dad promised he'd tuck me in and say goodnight.

He picked me up and flipped me over in the air. The ceiling turned into the floor, brilliantly lit by the living room chandelier. I wanted to walk through all those shimmers of glass, twinkly as fireflies. I kicked my feet. When Dad set me back down, I hugged his legs in a rush of mild drunkenness, trying not to lose my balance. I lifted my head and looked up into his eyes. Intensely hopeful, I asked him to stay the night at our house.

Dad burst out laughing. He knelt down to match my height and took my face into his enormous hands.

"I can't do that, sweetheart, because your grandparents haven't given me permission." He leaned closer and whispered into my ear: "Go ahead and brush your teeth and I'll be up in a minute."

I climbed the stairs as fast as I could, vaulting two and sometimes even three steps at a time, and I sped through my nightly ritual. I gargled several swigs of mouthwash that burned my gums where my new teeth were starting to peek through. Then I went to my bedroom to find my pajamas and wait for my father. I tried to wait patiently, sitting on the edge of the bed, but I couldn't stay still. My heart hammered in my chest. At the faintest hint of noise, I leapt under the covers and pretended to be asleep, because I wanted to open my eyes and startle my father with a sudden kiss on the cheek as soon as he leaned in to say goodnight. I repeated the feint a couple times, but I couldn't stand it any longer.

I decided to go get him and lead him upstairs myself.

As I scurried down the steps, I noted that someone had turned off the lights in the living room. The entrance hall was half-lit by the glow of the streetlamps filtering in through the windows. For a moment, I thought Dad must have left, or that the image of my parents chatting calmly over coffee had been a dream. The pain in my arm was still as fierce as if I'd submerged it in hot tar. My skin felt like when Dad rubbed his beard-scruff on my cheeks until they were as shiny as an ember dancing in the fire.

I heard murmurs, laughter.

I squinted to make out their silhouettes in the dim light. But a magnetic field arose between us. As much as I wanted to run and yell for them to come upstairs with me and put me to bed, something tugged at me from deep inside and held me back. Silently, I slipped closer and hid in one of the hallways that fed into the living room.

The murmurs were fading away and my parents' voices turned to clicks. As these damp noises shifted into ragged sighs, I found it harder and harder to breathe. The dense atmosphere in the living room drifted toward my hideout in waves and transported the smell of sweet burning wood. My arm's hot ache melted into the warmth and the gasps from the other side.

A stifled cry rose up from my mother's very core. I imagined her scratching at the sky.

I stuck my head out from behind the wall that separated us. The lioness was on the attack. My mother, her dress pulled up to her waist, was gripping my father with her legs. She grabbed one of his hands with great authority and guided him where she wanted him to touch her. She ran her hands over the head of her prey, combing her fingers through the tangle of gray and black hair until she reached his neck. She grabbed him as if she were strong enough to strangle him and sank her teeth into his flesh. I could see that my father's body wasn't resisting her at all; he writhed beneath her in rhythmic spasms. Then he burrowed his head between my mother's long legs and began to shake his head violently, scrubbing his beard against her skin, just as he did in our games.

I went back to my hiding place and lowered my head between my knees, curling around myself. I stuck my hands into my pajama pants and felt comforted by the heat and the damp. I closed my eyes tightly and started to sing a song in my head about a baby beluga in the deep blue sea, swimming so wild and swimming so free. I sang it again. And again. Faster and faster until the words stopped making sense.

In the distance, I heard my mother's anxious high-heeled footsteps and my father's keys jangling together.

Clicks and laughter.

The boom of the heavy metal door.

The hoarse rattle of Dad's car revving up on the other side of the window.

The screech of the tires on the pavement. Much like the sound that sprang out of me when I pulled my hands out of my clothes and realized that Dad had left my grandparents' house yet again without saying goodbye.

9

The carpet was rough, and the harder I struck it with my fists and legs, the coarser it felt. I didn't care if I scraped my elbows and knees. The friction was a spark that lit my lungs and ribs and released a raging battle cry. I didn't want a party. I didn't want magicians or clowns or kids in my house. Or cake or balloons or candles.

My mother's voice grew sharper and sharper. It cut into my new molars like the bit of an insistent, obnoxious drill, and every mention of getting ready for the big celebration made my nerves bristle. She came closer, trying to calm me down as I thrashed on the floor, shouting and crying. I jerked away from her. Whenever she stuck her lips to my cheeks, I recoiled at a bitter smell, as if her saliva were made of stagnant water from a forgotten vase. And her touch, cloying as the coppery perfume that saturated her neck, made me flail dizzily around on the rug.

Julia had brought María to the house very early on the day of the party. Before I was awake, Mom had already loaned her one of my dresses and drawn back her hair with an enormous yellow bow on top of her head. I couldn't help laughing when I saw her. Her arms looked stiff and uncomfortable, squeezed into the sleeves of a too-short, too-tight dress. She was still wearing sneakers, because she didn't have fancy shoes of her own and mine were three sizes too small. The whole outfit looked like a cocktail of colors and textures, and it clashed with her visible annoyance at the disguise she'd been forced into. She looked ridiculous. I stopped mocking her when I saw another dress, even stiffer and less comfortable than María's, hanging on the back of the door. Mom yanked it down over my body. With its three petticoat layers and sleeves reinforced with heavy shoulder pads spewing veils and more veils, the dress was a suit of armor that impeded me from moving at all. As soon as I had it on, my grandmother's shrill reproaches followed me all over the house, ordering me to be careful not to rip it.

I didn't want a dress. I didn't want cramped patent-leather shoes. I didn't want strange hairstyles. I didn't want any part in any ceremony that would force me to stay still, yielding rigidly to the camera like a wax doll. María, however, seemed thrilled with all these impostures, and paraded around as if the party were for her.

The guests would start to arrive within a couple of hours. Julia had cleared the living room and some of the first-floor rooms; they looked bigger and colder without furniture. My grandfather had hired a catering service, and the waiters hauled in long glass tables covered with appetizers; whenever María and I tried to sneak a Rice Krispies treat or a hot dog sliced into a flower, my grandmother appeared and gave us a smack on the hand, as if to shoo away a fly buzzing around the food.

One of the tables sported a mysterious box that two of the waiters had set down with special care. I asked María what she thought might be inside.

Dynamite?

The heart of a dove, ready to be transformed into a scarf inside the magician's hat?

Rabbits that would be released into the crowd and nibble the tablecloths?

We approached on tiptoe. Without a moment's hesitation, María lifted the cover off the box. Inside was the massive head of a smiling clown, covered in pastry cream and bits of chocolate. I felt an urge to plunge my finger deep into its pink nose. But before I could even raise my arm, my grandmother started to yell for us to get away from the table, that we were going to ruin the birthday cake Álvaro had brought, and she whisked it away.

That was when I threw myself onto the ground and started to scream.

My tears were a storm, and I wanted to sink the ship of the party. My grandmother went to find my mother. Mom answered my call and dashed over, flustered, clutching a banner to hang from the ceiling. She cajoled, promised me things, tried to console me—all useless. I was going to get my way even if I had to spend the rest of my life convulsing with rage on the floor. I was going to put a stop to this party.

She brought up my father: he was coming to celebrate, too, she reminded me. My fury blazed brighter at the thought that a whole week had passed since he'd left without saying goodnight. I sensed a trap. Mom, who seemed more excited about filling the piñata than answering my father's phone calls, was offering him to me as a reward if I calmed down and behaved. Ever since the night I'd seen them together, I felt that he was more interested in talking with her than with me. He kept calling the house and asking me to put her on the phone, and when I went to look for her, she ran into the bathroom or said to tell him she was busy, that she'd call him later. She'd grumble under her breath that he was crazy, and when I picked up the phone again to give him the message and keep regaling him with my news, he'd interrupt my stories about catastrophes or María and start asking after my mother, and beg me to do everything in my power to help him talk to her. And I'd look for her again and she'd run off again and the tragicomic choreography would continue until he'd give up and promise to come see me soon, but he never did. I wouldn't hear a word from him until the phone rang and their exasperating game of hunter-and-hunted started all over again.

María observed my tantrum impassively. Wasn't I embarrassed to have my friend see me crying like this? my mother whispered. She didn't know what else to do. She threatened to give away all my toys, to pinch me so hard I'd cry for real, to speed up the eclipse that would swallow up the earth, or to cancel the party altogether. The louder I screamed, the louder she threatened. We were like two ambulances blaring their haste to reach the disaster scene. As the minutes passed, I could see my mother's patience draining from her body. I felt powerful.

I wanted to provoke her. Challenge her to a duel I felt I'd already won.

She brought her face close to my ear again and begged me to stop making such a fuss. I looked her in the eye. My hand shot out to slap her, scratching the edge of her cheek.

A cold glow ignited her face. A taut silence stretched between us.

She stood up, smoothed her skirt, grabbed the banner—Welcome to My Party, it said—and left the room without a word.

10

The party dragged on. I liked tugging on the elastic band that rested under my chin and held up my pointed birthday hat, stretching it all the way down to my collarbone and then releasing it with a snap. I liked its flimsy whiplash, tickling me so that I was distracted from the throng of anonymous children gathered around to wish me happy birthday. Sometimes I rolled the rubber band around my finger until it turned purple. Or I placed the hat over my nose and transformed it into a beak that made me feel like one of the blackbirds, hidden away in my grandfather's study until the guests were gone.

A stranger lined us up in an uneven row. He ordered us to put our hands on the shoulders of the kid in front of us and pretend we were on a train. In neon overalls and an annoying falsetto, the man guided the group, rattling off popular platitudes and singing rounds for us to repeat in unison.

Under his command, we were ducks filing into the water.

Flimsy little puppets at the mercy of their strings, tugged this way and that.

Police.

Thieves.

Bad peg-legged pirates.

Statues.

Slimy French fries. Or at least the last ones to sit down were.

He decided when we could play, when we could eat,

and when we had to sit in silence to await the puppet show or the magic routine. Whenever I drifted out of the line he formed, or whenever I stayed still, observing the mass of strangers as they wriggled euphorically under his command, the man instantly called out my name and asked for a round of applause or cheers in my honor. He insisted that I had to be the most enthusiastic player in the game, the best-behaved little girl in the whole room, because it was my party and he wanted me to be all smiles at all times. I bared my teeth and threw dark glances at my mother, who was flirting with Álvaro and chatting with her friends.

He ordered us around like a sheepdog, but I rarely followed his instructions. I remember his voice taking on an edge of impatience every time he repeated himself, and he kept bringing his index finger to his mouth, asking us to shush, as if silence were an effective means of domesticating wild beasts. He needed to get us under control before the clowns arrived: the ones who were charged with revving up the raffle and distributing cake among the guests. Suspended above us was the huge bear-shaped piñata that my mother had fattened. I fantasized about reaching up and tugging on one of the strings that held its polystyrene belly together. I elbowed María, seated beside me, and flashed her a mischievous look to convey my plan through telepathy. She glanced upward and grinned. Then she covered her mouth with a finger, copying the man's gesture to keep quiet. I imagined myself deftly manipulating the cords hanging overhead. I wanted to yank them until the body burst and released an avalanche of confetti and little plastic toys that would bury the entertainer and all these unfamiliar children who were stuffing their cheeks with hot dogs and soda.

A sudden smack jerked me out of the paper tsunami I was devising in my head. My father greeted me with a loud kiss on the cheek and made room for himself among the guests to sit down beside me. Crossing his legs, he imitated how the rest of us were seated at the foot of the little stage. He looked like a giant in an assembly of leprechauns. He reached out and sat me down in his lap, shifting around restlessly as he asked if I was having fun, if I liked the party, if I'd made lots of new friends, what kinds of presents they'd given me—he didn't even pause for me to answer. Mute, I pulled off my birthday hat and placed it on his head, pulling firmly enough on the rubber band for it to cling to his restless jaw. The delicate band snapped as soon as it reached his neck, and Dad burst out laughing as all the kids stared at the man with oaky skin who had joined their circle.

He showered me with kisses and put his arm around me and whispered *Happy birthday*. He said I looked beautiful in my dress.

Then he fell silent.

He turned to focus on the back of the hall, on Mom and Álvaro. I saw his eyes fill with a dense haze that darkened his whole face. I felt his body tensing up under my petticoats, and I threw my arms around him, hard, as if clinging to a piece of driftwood in the current. Disentangling himself from me, he leapt to his feet and walked to the front, where the clowns were. He stormed up to the head clown, the one holding the microphone, and snatched it away from him. My father, the showman, puffed up his chest and started talking loudly into the mic.

Half-shouting, he sputtered into the microphone, spattering it with saliva, his voice marred by a low, faltering whistle as the sound cut out erratically. He introduced himself to a gathering of children who had no idea he was the father of Inés, queen of the party, and he demanded that everyone clap and cheer for me. He rambled and slurred to the indifferent audience—and then he raised his voice and shouted for them to be quiet. Looking out at the startled faces of the speechless crowd, he guffawed and asked me to join him in front.

Come on, sweetheart, come up here with the clowns. I stared as he waved his arms at me, and I winced, feeling a crackle of shame run through me, a violent surge that forbade me to stand. I tried to shake my head no, so that he'd see I didn't want to go, but a small hurricane was brewing in my belly, and I had to stay still: any sudden movement could make me vomit.

Dad jutted out a leg and leaned toward the group of kids. Like a human wall, we all inhaled sharply and leaned backward where we sat, arching away from the giant as he threatened to trip and collapse on top of us.

My father and his awkward gestures kept summoning me. *Come on, honey, come up here with your daddy.*

And he reached out his hand. But I stayed rooted there, petrified, eyes on the floor, as I felt the stares of all the other kids whose fathers weren't fairy-tale monsters. Their murmurs. Their judgment. And then a dry, mocking burst of laughter from María, which turned my eyes into a swamp of tears: hot with pride, stagnant, unable to stream freely down my cheeks.

Dad was a tightrope walker. He turned his back to us. He took long strides toward the other clown, who was clutching a wooden board as a prop, and pushed his face right up to the man's red rubber nose. He grabbed the clown by the wrist and seized the board with a menacing snarl. He turned around again, stumbled. A morbid smile cracked across his face. It was as if, for just a moment, he'd abandoned his body and caught a glimpse of the man he was, making a fool of himself before a group of terrified children.

He loomed over me again.

Get up, princess, and come with me so I'm not all by myself.

I closed my eyes and tightened my fists.

Sweetie, come on, don't be rude. You don't want a spanking, do you?

And as the *p* and the *k* crackled in the static of the microphone, my father raised the wooden board he'd taken from the clown and started hitting his own legs, simulating the smacks he'd give me if I kept ignoring him.

Then Dad took my arm and yanked me up. Now we were both standing before the bewildered kids, who still hadn't figured out whether my father was a clown without his makeup or a disoriented magician's assistant.

Let's go find Mommy and see if she loves us.

And he started off toward her, setting his hands down on various children's heads for support along the way. As he dodged chairs, he didn't notice that the microphone cable was tangled around his torso and legs like a snake. By the time he finally reached the back of the hall, I thought the audience might burst into applause. More than the tremulous steps of a drunk, the spectacle was a feat worthy of an acrobat.

Hey, princess, do you know that man with your mother? Why don't you introduce us . . . ?

Dad planted his left hand against the wall and leaned down to whisper into my mother's ear. He didn't seem to realize or care that the microphone amplified his whispers and turned them into breathy clicks echoing all over the room. Mom acted as if she had no idea what was going on and avoided his eyes. Enraged by her unresponsiveness, Dad raised his voice. My mother remained impassive, her gaze remote, until Dad took the wooden board and started to graze her knees with it. He brought the wooden edge up her leg, slowly, lifting the hem of her short skirt, exposing a thigh-level run in her stocking. As he traveled her skin with the board, my mother's shoulders stiffened like they always did when my grandfather shouted at her. Her breathing quickened and her lower lip trembled like a tuning fork.

"Javier, please, that's enough," she said, without lifting her eyes. "Can't you see that Inés is waiting for us to cut Álvaro's cake?"

Mom got up and stepped toward the group of children still sitting on the floor. She placed her hands on a couple of their shoulders. Sweetly, she asked them to line up at the main table, because it was time for cake. And then.

11

The main hall became a battlefield.

An enormous Mickey Mouse, shaking his head to the music and miming ineptly, set out to clear the floor of grown-ups so the skirmish could begin. The entertainer lined up several chairs in the middle of the hall and explained to us, in rhymes and cheap jokes, that this was the territory we'd have to conquer through dance. The logistics of the war were very simple. We would walk in a circle around the chairs, stalking each other as silent jaguars hunt their prey. As soon as the music stopped, we'd have to rush over and claim one of the seats as our own. If you didn't manage to sit down, you lost, and you'd have to trudge away in humiliation and defeat—and the next round there would be one chair fewer. If you survived all the rounds, you'd be crowned lord and master of the party, winning a massive stuffed rabbit wrapped in cellophane that the clowns displayed like the grand prize on a game show.

María was on the other side of the hall. She was dancing with my father, her feet riding on top of his, and she laughed at his clumsiness. I was the one who'd taught her to dance. Now she'd usurped me. I remembered the derisive chime of her laughter when my father had called me to the front, and I felt a visceral scream rising up from my belly, inciting me to lunge at her, wrest her away from him. I started to growl and salivate. My mission was to win the battle, vanquish María, distance her from my father, and make her cry in front of all the strangers at the party.

When the competition began, I transformed into Inés, warrior. Inés, saber-toothed tiger. Inés, perfectly aimed blow.

I used my agility and sharp nails to defeat my challengers one by one. I devised a technique: I skirted the chairs, barely grazing them with my fingertips, as I bounced my shoulders to the rhythm of Las Chicas del Can. When the music stopped, I pressed my hand against the plastic surface and gained traction to leap forth and seize the chair. If an opponent dared to dispute my territory, I had no qualms about biting or elbowing him out of the way. And so I proceeded to trounce each and every one of my guests—until only María and a single chair remained. I'd have to fight her to the death.

Like a prelude to the grand finale, the clowns called all the kids to gather round and watch the competition. They took each of us by the arm and introduced us to the audience like a pair of boxers. In one corner, María, all smiles, with the quickest curls in the West. In the other, Inés, the birthday girl, ready to harness the titanic strength of her seven years on earth and take down her rival.

And the music started to play.

I couldn't take my eyes off María. I wanted to intimidate her. I wanted her to realize that I was challenging her to a duel in which my honor and my father's were at stake. No one else was allowed to dance with him like that anywhere, much less at my own party. She returned my stare and defiantly furrowed her brow. I responded with a shrill bark and pressed my hand into the chair, waiting intently for the music to stop. To increase the suspense, the entertainer bluffed, postponing the moment of truth, speeding up and slowing down the songs so that we'd match the rhythm as he manipulated it. To me, nothing mattered but María—nothing else was even there. Not the hands of the grown-ups, clapping to the music; not my mother's cheers from the sideline; not the clowns' soccer-match commentary. I was utterly concentrated on claiming that chair, which gleamed before me like a trunk full of provisions on the shore of a deserted island.

The hall went still. And María and I lunged at each other.

12

I slammed into a polar cap. A wall of ice smashed against my ribs and hurled me to the floor: the sharp bones of María's hips felling me just as I'd managed to sit half my body down onto the chair. She shoved me hard and sent me flying far from the grand prize. Sprawled on the ground, I could barely make out the clowns' shrill voices as they demanded a round of applause for my friend. I vaulted to my feet as if my spine were a spring and ignored the pain shooting through my wrists. I gathered momentum and charged at her. My hands turned into a venomous scorpion stinger, and I gave her a pinch that radiated all the fury I felt seething in my stomach. María wouldn't stand for that: she reached out and yanked at my hair. My nails had branded her arm, but she still clung to the stuffed rabbit she'd won in our faceoff.

"Give it to me, María, it's mine!"

"Stop it, Inés! I won, not you."

"No way. You cheated."

"I did not! My daddy taught me that cheating is bad. I'm not like you."

"Shut up, you stupid maid!"

And as these words flew out of me, hateful as pebbles in a peashooter, the tears pooled in my eyes began to melt, sliding down my cheeks and coming to rest on my tongue. Without a second thought, I gathered a dense mouthful of swampy saliva and spat it right into her face. But she dodged the projectile, which landed on the nose of the stuffed rabbit we both coveted. I snatched away the toy and hugged it close to protect it from her wily claws. But María grasped me under the armpits and tickled me fiercely until I had no choice but to release my prey.

A mob of kids and grown-ups had gathered around to watch us fight, astonished. For a moment, I was flooded with a light, rapturous rage. I felt that they were the audience at a circus and hungered for a show, so I spat at them, too, and dialed up my tantrum. Spattered with my sticky drool, the crowd drew back. But I carried on in my destructive trance, spinning around the hall like a tiny tornado.

My grandmother appeared before me. She clenched her teeth. Smiling tersely, she asked me to calm down. I swung my arms around with greater force, as if they'd turned into the blades of a helicopter, ready to demolish her. She only repeated that she'd had enough, that I had to be quiet, that I shouldn't make her look worse in front of our guests. That I shouldn't be such a brat. Furtively, she pinched me on the side to teach me a lesson.

I stopped whirling and doubled over with pain.

From that angle, I saw my father's legs hurrying over to us, his mottled hands pushing away my grandmother.

Just like that, everyone became enemies in a soap opera that sprang to life before my eyes. Shouts and insults. Dad and my grandmother argued, lobbing words back and forth in a ping-pong skirmish. Their growls were joined by the roars of the half-drunk beast, and they shouted so furiously that neither side could hear what the other was saying. My mother tried in vain to separate them. Their slurs and snarls tangled into a wild mass with no beginning or end.

From the corner of my eye, I glimpsed María creeping toward the rabbit, which had been abandoned on a table at the back of the hall. I think my mother was the one who'd put it there, far away from me, thinking naively that I'd stop fighting if the prize were removed from my field of vision. María, meanwhile, was glancing craftily from side to side and approaching the spoils. She'd taken advantage of my distraction with the grown-ups to pilfer the reward that was mine by right. I got down on all fours and made my way toward my opponent. I had to prevent this plunder.

The white noise stirred up by Dad, Mom, and my grandparents' clamoring voices abruptly stopped. The beast growled something about getting my father out of his house even if it meant a bullet to the head and stalked off to the study. My grandfather's thick voice took up almost as much space as the heavy air filling the hall. With his departure, silence returned. Until my father took a deep breath and imitated my grandmother's grimace. And then, like the foghorn of a ship as it cuts through the haze, his words disrupted the calm:

"Of course, I smell like shit because I'm broke. Frigid old bitch!"

Javier, relax, buddy.

Álvaro's voice chafed through the hall like claws on a blackboard. I felt it reverberating inside my mouth. It made me clamp down on my newly loosening teeth. I shot him a scornful glance, hoping that his crack at diplomacy would be useless. I needed the grown-up fight to continue so I could crawl invisibly over to María and deliver the single slap that would win me back my rabbit.

Álvaro approached my father, speaking in an affable, conciliatory tone. Beside him, Dad didn't look so tall, and the prominent belly on my mother's boyfriend made my father look gaunt. Dad tried to shake him off, but Álvaro's grip on his arm was stronger. Stealthily, I shifted my elbows and knees over the floor, which was grimy now with traces of the party. I calculated the distance separating me from the girl who dared to claim what was mine.

Why don't I show you the door?

And just as Álvaro tugged at my father's arm with the intention of escorting him out, I pounced on María and snatched the rabbit from her hands. My upward leap from the floor was so powerful that, when I pushed her, she tripped on one of the cables hooked up to the amplifier, and the only thing that broke her fall was the sharp glass edge of a table. Her head smashed into the corner. The blow was thunderous: the crystal teardrops of the chandelier trembled so hard that they clattered into each other. Then there was no sound in the hall but the tinkling of the glass.

Or maybe it was María's skull as it cracked.

Within seconds, a weak stream of blood became a scarlet pool that flooded the marble floor. If I close my eyes, I can still see the brilliance of that russet lake under my black patent-leather shoes, which were shiny, too.

13

Inés. What happened? Inés.

My mother's voice was as distant as a siren song. My mind was frozen, and so were the words I needed to explain why María was on the ground. Captive to the urgent instinct that had spared her so many catastrophes, my mother knelt beside María and gently lifted her head. She assessed the wound and lay a cloth over it to stop the bleeding. And she asked Julia, whose face had drained of color at the sight of her unconscious granddaughter, to bring a first aid kit and some cleaning supplies for the floor. Dad approached Mom and asked how he could help; he reminded her that he knew a little first aid, too. Mom glared at him. But after a long pause, she said that if he really wanted to feel useful, he could take María to the emergency room. Álvaro, seconding the idea, offered to call a cab and even chip in for the fare—anything to get my father out of the house.

The beast bellowed from the top of the stairs, oblivious to everything that had happened with María. Disoriented by my grandmother's shouts as she begged him to stay put—all that mattered now was getting the girl to the hospital—he stormed downstairs, sputtering insults, and he only stopped when he'd come all the way over to us. He rubbed his rifle's wooden handle with his claws and looked steadily at my father. He wore a macabre smile. He salivated. He wanted to swallow my father up in a single gulp and suck the marrow from every bone.

The gun jostled from side to side in the beast's trembling paws. It was as if the rifle had turned into a prosthetic arm, charged and powerful, ready to lash out at anyone who didn't conform to his every whim. Its muzzle looked like the bottom of a deep, dark well, and I wanted to get close enough to finally see my reflection there. Fearful, narcissistic, I fantasized about what sort of shape might peer up from the darkness of the gun. All the secrets I needed to know about the end of the world, I was sure, would be found at the bottom of that barrel. I felt an urge to touch it, and I took a step forward, but Mom swiftly yanked me back.

We looked like a group of odalisques trying to sneak out while the tyrant sleeps. We calculated the beast's exhalations, gauged every movement, even tried not to blink—all to avoid offending him. Anything that could be read as a peace overture might rekindle his fury and release his clumsily loaded cartridges. We tracked the beast's perverse gestures from where we stood. My father's heavy, anxious breathing was a hoarse croak that filled the hall. The beast looked thrilled at my father's palpable fear, the way he covered his face to keep from looking the beast in the eye, all but sobbing. Every whimper, every birdlike tremor sent the beast into a fit of cackling, and he stroked his rifle with satisfaction. My father offered no resistance at all: he responded to every jeer with a sound more like a whistle than a word.

But something about the scene was out of focus. Instead of aiming the gun at my father with assurance and skill, the beast looked like a little boy playing cowboys and Indians with a broomstick. He brandished the weapon hamfistedly in his drunken stupor, unable to gather his pudgy fingers around the trigger. Mom sensed that the major threat wasn't his masterful marksmanship but his incompetence. She walked up to him, resolute.

"What exactly do you plan to do with that, Dad?" my mother hissed, as if scolding a mischievous child. She seized the rifle by the barrel and pushed it toward the floor as easily as she'd handle a trinket, a toy. There's nothing weaker than the residue of a stubborn whim. "Javier, your taxi is here. Call us as often as you can to let us know how María is doing."

The beast's eyes flashed with rage and he snarled. I shrank back toward my father and hugged him around the legs, terrified that the beast would attack him in one of his unpredictable outbursts. But neither Julia nor my grandmother seemed to be responding to his threats; they were busy with the tasks my mother had assigned them in our makeshift hospital. Confronted with the indifference of his subjects and my mother's stern stare, my grandfather let out one last shuddering exhalation and dropped the gun. And he turned and slunk out of the room, a tired, defeated animal.

I wanted to throw my arms around my father's waist, but he moved away from me. I couldn't know it at the time, but the earth was already shifting, already splitting underfoot. The deep chasm that would cleave open between us was barely visible then. The distance between his body and my arms was just the first inkling of his absence. He crouched down next to María, who still hadn't woken up, and carefully placed his hands behind her head to support her neck. He lifted her up with a broad smile and crooned sweetly to her, as if they were a pair of newlyweds crossing the threshold of a new home where a life of togetherness awaited. I lifted my arms, too, expecting my father to take me with him. Then

I lowered my eyes and saw Dad reflected in the dense pool of blood, leaving without saying goodbye once more. I took a deep breath and closed my eyes. Maybe it was a fortune-teller's fleeting epiphany that made me open them again, wanting another glimpse of my father's silhouette in that crimson swamp. He'd leave María and come back for me and we'd go away together, far away, once and for all. But when I looked back at the mirrored stain, he was gone. The lake only reflected my legs, which were shaking uncontrollably, and the glimmering of the great chandelier overhead.

I lay down in the pool. I flailed my limbs, venturing a couple of strokes and kicks to confirm my amphibian self. Maybe, if he saw me swimming, Dad would come back to me.

14

On the night my father left with María, the end of the world was announced.

On the radio, at least: broadcasters discussed the eclipse that promised to switch off the sun the next day. An expert's timorous voice carefully explained how the moon, the earth, and the sun would all line up in a row, and for a few seconds it would be nighttime in the middle of the day. She talked about Chinese astronomers who were decapitated when they couldn't rationally explain this phenomenon that so startled the emperor. The only thing we absolutely must not do during the eclipse, she stressed several times, was look directly into the sky.

I imagined the sound of the sun shutting off as I waited for my father. I couldn't decide whether the eclipse would be accompanied by the wild thunder of the smothered star or the hushed murmur of the wind blowing through a night that would never fade into dawn again. I imagined deserted midday beaches illuminated only by moonlight, vast and intensely white, moments before it was all over. I imagined the dark guts of the mountains as the sun exploded, turning everything that wasn't countryside into mud and lime. I imagined the rain drying up just before it fell indifferently to the barren soil, and I imagined a troop of restless animals trying to clamber over the edges of the earth. My fear-coated landscapes planted themselves under my eyelids as I fought to stay awake, waiting for my father to return.

My eyes burned with the desire to see him again. I

rubbed them fiercely. My gaze clouded over with irides-
cent worms wriggling around, which I found so alarming
that I closed my eyes again and waited for them to fade
away in their perverse transparency. I took a long, deep
breath. Everything would be fine in just a few hours,
when Dad came back. I imagined reaching out for his
rough hands. I'd bring them to my face, suck on his fingers, ask him to read me the parts of the encyclopedia
that named every kind of dinosaur that had ever walked
the earth. When we were together, we'd walk through the
countryside and collect strange rocks and false four-leaf
clovers and I'd store them away as treasure. At nightfall,
we'd lie down on the soft bed of pine needles behind his
house and eat chocolate. We'd gingerly peel away the foil
wrappers and remove the little sheets attached to them,
the prizes: on one side were portraits of polar bears,
wolves, wild foxes, hares, and whales, and on the other
side, the animal's scientific name and a brief description
of its behavior. Dad would firmly pronounce *Ursus mari-
timus* or *Canis lupis* and recite the predators' mammalian
habits while I'd nestle sleepily into his neck and feel the
warm rise and fall of his breath.

Then we'd wait for the eclipse. He'd set me on his
shoulders and ask me not to look directly into the sky.
He'd carefully adjust my intergalactic visor and encour-
age me to open my eyes. Just as the sun started to burn
out, Dad would tighten his grip on my knees and wouldn't
let me fall.

I fell asleep to the thought that maybe, just maybe, I
wouldn't fear the end of the world once he was with me.

15

I didn't have to wait long. Early the next morning, Mom asked me to shower with her to save time. Her urgency only confirmed my suspicions that I'd be reunited with my father sooner rather than later. I remember that day because I felt very happy to be there with her. I watched her, half-hypnotized, as she soaped me up and rinsed me off. The water surged down onto her head and streamed over her breasts with the strength of a river plunging off a cliff, transformed into a cascade. My mother, suddenly a formidable geological accident, seemed oblivious to the torrent fringing her body as she hummed songs about women who promised never to fall in love again or who got caught out in the rain. I lowered my eyes and lamented that the water didn't rebound against my own torso, which was so flat that it looked more like a listless rectangle than an awe-inspiring mountain. Maybe it was this telluric power that made my father want so badly to be near her. Me, I was just a flat animal. Inés, vertical worm, forced to build her house by the mountain, resigned to never being the mountain herself.

I slithered through the dense, warm fog that drifted out from the shower and made my way to the bedroom, spattering the floor with the water that slipped off my body. Mom energetically rubbed her legs and shoulders with the towel and then wrapped it around her head like a turban. Pointing her toes like spearheads, she rolled her stockings to create holes she could stick her feet into.

She asked me to start dressing myself, because we were getting picked up in less than an hour.

Mom had laid out my clothes for the day. But I didn't want to get dressed. I balled them up and tossed them across the room. I felt free in my nakedness. I climbed onto the bed and started to jump. I felt the water droplets vanishing with every bound. The larva was viscous no longer: now it had wings. I cawed every time the mattress flung me upward. I was sister to the blackbirds. I strained upward in an attempt to touch the ceiling and I felt the blood coursing through me, burning my feather-stripped arms.

I was Inés, bird, ready to embark on my northern migration, ready to fly away with my father.

Impatient, Mom grabbed my feet and stuffed them into my shoes. She brusquely lifted my arms and everything went dark: she'd covered my head with a cotton sweater. *I've been asking you all morning to be quick and you're not listening to me.* I struggled to make out my mother's words; the sleeves hung beside my ears. *Finish up now. It's time to go.*

"Are Dad and María coming back yet?" I asked eagerly.

Before she could respond, we heard my grandmother's voice on the other side of the door. The car was here, she said, and we had to hurry. And now that Julia wasn't here, someone had to cover the blackbirds in the kitchen so that they wouldn't panic at the false night heralded by the eclipse.

Mom bent down and brought her face close to mine. Gently: *Hurry up and finish getting dressed, sweetie, so we can see what's going to happen in the sky*, and she opened the bedroom door.

My mother smiled as a pair of huge leather shoes timidly stepped in.

I lifted my face, expecting to look into the river-fish eyes of my father. But it wasn't him. Álvaro stood before me instead. He took a few steps closer and gave me an awkward pat on the head, as if he were petting a dog.

"Where's Dad?" I asked my mother, confused.

Mom ignored my question and turned away. She put her arms around Álvaro's back and kissed his neck. I heard the blackbirds screeching anxiously in the background, disoriented as the dark cloak of night began to envelop them in the middle of the day.

16

I ran into the kitchen, wanting to take charge of the neglected birds in their cage. And there was María. She calmly observed the blackbirds' anarchic flapping, standing stock-still as they rattled their bodies against the rusty bars. I walked over to her and opened the cage door so the blackbirds could flee the chaos. It took them a moment to realize they were free. Then they shot out and careened wildly around the kitchen. I chased them through the house. My own wingbeats collided with the walls, the hallways. It was a filament of sound that threaded and unraveled as we traveled through the labyrinth.

The heavy metal door in the distance—if I could manage to get it open, both the blackbirds and I would be free.

I shoved with all my strength and winked at María to follow me. I let out a roar so powerful that it shuddered the glass tears suspended from all the chandeliers in the house.

We were out. The girls and the birds, single file, as darkness began to stain the sky.

I was barefoot and the asphalt burned my soles. The only way to reach the street and start looking for my father, who couldn't be far away yet, was to become Inés, panther. Inés, hunter of large game, feline of thick fur. Tiny bits of gravel clung to my hands and knees. Rearing back, I gathered enough momentum to spring into the middle of the road, where Dad should be. But I couldn't see him anywhere. The city's sudden silence seeped into my ears and made me dizzy.

I roared again to interrupt the hush.

I raised my hands to protect myself from the sun and looked both ways. Maybe I'd just lost sight of him for an instant.

I had to be sure.

As Inés, quadruped, I advanced a few more meters until I reached a lamppost. Resting at its base were a couple of large trash bags, and I barked loudly at them, just in case my father was inside. But no one was there: only a pair of pigeons lurking among some scattered scraps of food, scared off by the racket I'd made. Now they were perched on a telephone line. I bellowed to startle them.

It wasn't yet dark. Shards of glass shimmered on the pavement like an oasis. The mirage rippled the street and I felt as if I were kneeling on a frozen lake just before it thawed. My feet began to tremble on the pavement and I thought they might turn into a material as liquid as the ground I stood on. I was afraid.

Trying to keep myself together, I rubbed my hands and knees on the asphalt and felt miniscule pebble-bits stick to my skin. The pinching burn diluted my dizziness and made me feel rooted to the pavement.

My body kept shaking, but I stayed down on all fours.

A shadow started to swallow everything up. I wanted that darkness to gulp me down, too, as it slowly devoured the sky. I may have been a wild animal, but I still felt restless. I let out a roar from the very back of my throat and gathered enough strength to stand upright. I needed a broader view of all the places where my father might be hiding, and I started to turn around and around like a cat chasing its tail.

I held out my arms. My surroundings blurred into a uniform smear as I whirled. If I spun in circles, I thought, everything around me might be magically put back together when I stopped, like a jigsaw puzzle assembled at my whim.

The possibilities were infinite.

I heard my mother shouting in the distance, asking me to stop, or maybe telling me that Dad had arrived. Álvaro hovered beside her like a ghost. I stopped and felt the blood surging to my head. The vertigo made my body go slack and light, and I jerked from side to side, trying to find my center. I walked a few meters away from the house and saw a silhouette pointing upward, showing me the sky. Finally, my father was here. But his body dissolved among the curious bystanders who had emerged from their houses to watch, and I lost him in the crowd. The day went darker and I remembered the warnings on the radio: during the eclipse, no one should look directly into the sun.

Everything went silent. The sun had turned into a half-moon and the false night enveloped us. Dad was nowhere to be found. He had failed me. The moon continued along its course and there was one last tiny flash of light before the sun switched off altogether. The end of the world had arrived, and my father wasn't here to receive it with me. We weren't going to be accessories or witnesses to the disaster.

Without raising my eyes, I threw myself onto the nearest body, as if I were some sort of inverse prey surrendering to the jaws of her predator. I wanted to hug this man around the neck, wanted him to take me someplace where we could start a new life. Where we could observe the end of time. He would be a new father, the promise of a new home. But I didn't find the warmth of a hug. Only the image of two warped and bloodied feet with a sack of broken glass beside them. I leaned closer to give him a kiss and ask him to take me away with him, but as I drew closer, I felt the sour breath of a different mammal. I looked into his gray eyes and saw his snout twist into an uneasy grimace. I realized that this strange wolf didn't want to be my father, either. He shook me off with a rough paw and I fell to the pavement.

I lifted my head until the sun's slender halo stroked my hair. I bared my teeth and opened my eyes. I wasn't afraid to look straight into the sky.

Acknowledgments

I'd like to thank Alejandro Gómez Dugand, Andrés Burgos, and Alejandra Algorta for helping me shape this story. My gratitude to Giuseppe Caputo, Catalina Arango, Camilo Jaramillo, Camilo Jiménez, Mónica Palacios, and Juan José Richards for reading and responding to my many drafts. Thanks, too, to Adriana Martínez for meticulously editing this book in the original Spanish, and to Amalia Andrade, Ximena Gama, and María Fernanda Prieto for their continuous encouragement.

Diego Esquivel, Gloria González, and Ana María Esquivel, thank you for believing that my stories would always see me through.